WARRIOR'S CHOICE

"What should I do?" Touch the Sky asked Arrow Keeper. "I am a *Shaiyena.* But my white parents are the soul of my medicine bag. How can I let these things happen to them?"

"Do you realize what the rest will think and say if you desert your tribe now? And, little brother, have you considered Honey Eater? She loves you. But Black Elk loves her. When her father dies, she will need you more than ever. She will be alone. A Cheyenne who is alone is a dead Cheyenne."

Touch the Sky's heart felt heavy as a stone. Arrow Keeper was telling him that Honey Eater would almost surely have to marry Black Elk if Touch the Sky were gone too long.

"Do you go to help the whites who raised you, knowing it may turn your tribe against you forever and cost you Honey Eater?" Arrow Keeper asked. "Or do you stay?"

The *Cheyenne* Series:

#1: ARROW KEEPER
#2: DEATH CHANT

RENEGADE JUSTICE

JUDD COLE

LEISURE BOOKS  NEW YORK CITY

A LEISURE BOOK®

January 1993

Published by

Dorchester Publishing Co., Inc.
276 Fifth Avenue
New York, NY 10001

Printed in the United States of America.

Prologue

When the short white days of the cold moons had ended, Running Antelope of the Northern Cheyennes and his party of 30 braves were ambushed near the North Platte by Bluecoat pony soldiers.

Running Antelope was a peace leader, not a war chief, and his band flew a white truce flag. His wife Lotus Petal and their infant son accompanied him in order to visit her Southern clan. Badly outnumbered, the Cheyennes sang their battle song and fought bravely with their bows, lances, clubs, and single-shot muzzle-loaders. But they were no match for the Bluecoats' thundering wagon guns and percussion-cap carbines. The lone survivor of the bloody assault was the squalling Cheyenne orphan.

The child was taken back to the river-bend settlement of Bighorn Falls near Fort Bates in the

Wyoming Territory. Raised by John and Sarah Hanchon, owners of the town's mercantile store, he was named Matthew. Despite occasional hostile glances and remarks from some whites, he grew up feeling accepted in his narrow world.

Then came 1856, his sixteenth year, and tragedy: Matthew's forbidden love for Kristen Steele, daughter of the wealthiest rancher in Bighorn Falls. A jealous young officer from Fort Bates, Seth Carlson, eager to win Kristen's hand in marriage, threatened to ruin John Hanchon's contract with the fort unless Matthew cleared out for good.

The saddened youth left his white parents and rode north into the upcountry of the Powder River, hostile Cheyenne country, determined to find a place where he fit in. Captured by Cheyenne braves from Chief Yellow Bear's camp, he was accused of being a double-tongued spy for the whites. He was sentenced to death by torture.

Only the intervention of old Arrow Keeper, the tribal medicine man, spared him. The shaman recognized the birthmark, buried past the youth's hairline, from a recent and powerful medicine vision: a mulberry-colored arrowhead, the mark of the warrior. Arrow Keeper hoped it was not a false vision placed over his eyes by his enemies. If true, this young buck was destined to lead his people in a great, victorious battle against their enemies.

Renamed Touch the Sky by Arrow Keeper, the tall youth was hated by the rest of the tribe, especially a stern warrior named Black Elk and his bitter young cousin, Wolf Who Hunts Smiling. Black Elk was stung by jealousy when he realized that Chief Yellow Bear's daughter, Honey

Eater, loved Touch the Sky instead of him. And Wolf Who Hunts Smiling openly walked between Touch the Sky and the campfire—the Cheyenne way of announcing his intention to kill the suspected spy.

Touch the Sky bravely and cunningly employed his white friend Corey Robinson in a bold plan to save the Cheyenne village from annihilation by Pawnees. He was honored in a special council, and Honey Eater secretly declared her love for him. But he was still far from full acceptance as a warrior.

Then whiskey traders invaded Indian country. Once again Touch the Sky was suspected of spying for the long knives—the traders tricked him into getting drunk with them, convincing his angry friend Little Horse that he was one of them. The traders, led by the ruthless Henri Lagace, threatened to rapidly destroy the Indian way of life with their strong water.

But Lagace didn't stop at peddling devil water. He and his men were also fond of getting Indians and other white traders drunk, then slaughtering them in their sleep and robbing them—and making the massacres look like Cheyenne handiwork. The panicked Territorial Commission declared a bounty on the scalp of any and all Cheyennes.

The peace-loving Chief Yellow Bear knew his warriors had to paint their faces for war against Lagace if the Cheyennes were to survive. But Lagace kidnapped Yellow Bear's daughter. He threatened to kill Honey Eater if the war was not called off.

Yellow Bear could not sacrifice the tribe to spare Honey Eater. The only hope was to send a small Cheyenne war party, led by Black Elk, into the heavily fortified white stronghold. Touch the Sky was told, in a medicine vision, that he must defy Black Elk or Honey Eater would die. He deserted the war party and infiltrated the white camp on his own.

Taken prisoner, he was brutally tortured. But his courage in defying the whites rallied the other Cheyennes to mount an heroic surprise assault. They scattered the whites and freed Honey Eater. Touch the Sky then pursued his enemy Lagace across the plains until he killed him, ending the scalps-for-bounty decree and the immediate threat to the Cheyennes.

But much of his valor went unwitnessed. Many of his enemies within the tribe were still unconvinced of his loyalty. He was still trapped between the white man's hatred and the red man's mistrust.

Chapter One

"Shorten the reins, Wade!" shouted John Hanchon. "You want to control his head!"

Hanchon was perched on the top pole of a corral so new it still reeked of fresh pine. He was a thickset, middle-aged man wearing a broad-brimmed plainsman's hat, sturdy linsey trousers, and calfskin boots.

He watched his foreman expertly snub the reins so the mean roan bronco couldn't get its head down for some serious bucking.

"Some horses hate the saddle, others save it for the rider," he explained to the two men flanking him on the corral pole. "Each horse bucks to its own pattern. You don't try to power a strong pattern bucker. You learn to feel it coming and ride with the motion."

The three men watched the roan futilely side-jump a few more times before it finally gave up and stood defeated, its bit flecked with foam. A cheer rose from the rest of the hands scattered around the corral. This was the spring's first "Sunday ronnyvoo" at John and Sarah Hanchon's new mustang spread, and a festive spirit hung in the air.

"You got a fine spread here, Mr. Hanchon," said Corey Robinson, a freckle-faced redhead with a gap-tooth grin. He was 16, the youngest of the trio seated on the corral pole. "I wish to Jesus my pa would get out of the preaching business so we could start us a spread. It ain't just Fort Bates that needs remounts. Seems as how every keelboat crew that comes past Bighorn Falls is looking for good horses and mules to take out west with them."

"Sure, there's good money in it," said the third man, Corey's friend Tom Riley. He was a brevet officer, an enlisted man temporarily promoted from the ranks until more commissioned lieutenants arrived at nearby Fort Bates. He was 20, a rangy, clean-cut towhead whose face was sunburned where the black brim of his officer's hat turned up on one side. "But it's damn hard work breaking green horses to leather."

"Speak the truth, lad, and shame the devil," said Hanchon. "And it takes money to make money. Sure, my herds are grazing the new grass now. But I had to hay them all winter long. It took everything I made from selling the mercantile just to weather the cold."

"It ain't fair," said Corey. His freckles stood out even more as he flushed with anger. "It's bad enough that Hiram Steele drove Matthew off like he was a killer coyote hanging around the henhouse. There was no call for running you out of business."

At the mention of his adopted Cheyenne son, the seams in Hanchon's face deepened. He still didn't know exactly what had passed, nearly one year ago now, between Matthew and the wealthy rancher Hiram Steele. Whatever it was, it somehow involved Steele's daughter. And it had been serious enough to send Matthew packing for good in the middle of the night. Though his good-bye note made it clear he was leaving to protect his adopted white parents, his departure still hadn't been enough for Hiram Steele—he and friends at Fort Bates had conspired to turn the once-friendly fort sutler against Hanchon. When orders from the fort began going to the mercantile at Red Shale, Hanchon's mercantile in Bighorn Falls was doomed.

" 'Fair' don't mean spit to a man like Steele," said Hanchon bitterly. "I was doing tolerable well until he ruined me. But I'm plumb bullheaded when I get my dander up. That's why I started this mustang spread. Oh, I knew there'd be trouble. I knew Steele wouldn't set still for this. He's the kind that always figures there's too many pigs for the tits. Still, I never marked him down for a common criminal. My hand to God, I thought he'd get used to the notion of another spread in this valley. So far I'm wrong."

Hanchon pointed toward one corner of the house, where the wood was badly charred.

"A while back, riders came in the night and tried to burn us out. All winter long, I found mustangs in my herds that'd been shot dead. My hands have been dry-gulched and beaten. It's gettin' to be the devil's own work just to keep enough help around here."

It was the spring of 1857. Up in the higher

country the golden aspens were coming to leaf, and the winter ice no longer had the valleys locked. Hanchon and his men had recently moved the mustang herds out from their nearby winter range to an outlying summer range dotted with new hayricks.

The Hanchon spread was located in a fertile piece of bottom land where the Tongue River oxbowed just south of Bighorn Falls in the Wyoming Territory. The split-log house was surrounded by a raw plank bunkhouse and outbuildings, two huge pole corrals, a stone well, and a long stone watering trough.

"Good lands!" said a cheerful female voice behind them. "Men surely do love to raise the dust!"

All three men turned around to a pleasant sight: Sarah Hanchon, her copper hair pulled into a tight bun, looked gay and lively in a bright yellow gingham dress. The young beauty at her side, Kristen Steele, smiled shyly when Corey and Tom hastily jumped down off the fence and touched the brims of their hats. She wore a dark calico skirt and a white shirtwaist. China-blue eyes were offset by a golden waterfall of hair tumbling down over her shoulders.

"Miss Steele," said John Hanchon, smiling with obvious pleasure at seeing her. In his book, Hiram's daughter was as pleasant and decent as her father was mean and low-down. No wonder that Matthew had fallen in love with her—what healthy young sprout wouldn't?

"I can't stay long," she said apologetically. "Pa would have a conniption if he knew I was here. But I wanted to see your new place."

A horse whickered loudly, capturing everyone's

attention. They all turned to watch a hired hand rope a white mustang and lead it into the horse-breaking pen. First the hand carefully checked his saddle, cinches, latigos, and stirrups. Then he examined the halter and rein. The horse had already been choked and water-starved until it could be saddled and harnessed. Finally the hand cinched on the bronc saddle and swung up into leather.

Cheers and shouts rose from the rest of the hands as the rider put spurs to his mount and rode it with his rowels until the bucking mustang rolled its eyes in fury, showing the whites.

A moment later a rifle spoke its piece, and the mustang collapsed as a scarlet rope of blood erupted from its flank.

"God-in-whirlwinds!" said Corey.

Suddenly the air was alive with more gun-shots, the hollow thunder of hooves. From a long, sloping rise behind the house, a group of six marauders bore down on the gathering. Their faces were hidden behind bandanas.

A claybank horse crumpled, whickering piteously, as a bullet caught it in the hindquarters. More slugs thwacked into the corral poles, raised plumes of dust, flew past their ears with a sound like angry hornets.

"You two!" Hanchon shouted to his wife and Kristen as he scrambled down from the corral pole. "Into the house!"

It was Sunday, and the only man carrying a weapon was Riley. He unsnapped his stiff leather holster and drew the silver-gripped Colt service revolver.

Some of the hands were already running toward the bunkhouse for their weapons. But the attackers, anticipating this, laid down a withering field of fire between the corral and the bunkhouse. Two hands went down, wounded, before Wade McKenna shouted out the order to take cover instead.

Hanchon had fled into the house with the women. Now he burst back out through the leather-hinged door, a .33-caliber breechloader in one hand, a lever-action Henry in the other.

"Corey! Heads up, boy!"

Hanchon tossed the breechloader to the youth. Riley had already taken cover behind the stone watering trough, taking aim. He was reserving his ammunition until the attackers were within short-arms range.

A yellow cloud of dust boiled up behind the riders. Wood chips flew from the corral poles and outbuildings; another horse whickered in pain and went down. The other horses had panicked, and now their shrill nickering added to the din of shouts and gunshots.

Hanchon, standing in the open, fired the long-barreled Henry. One of the attackers slumped in his saddle but hung on, one hand covering the wound in his thigh.

"Cover down!" shouted Riley to Hanchon, jumping up and dragging the older man behind the trough with him and Corey. Now the attackers were within easy range, and all three men returned fire in earnest.

Another marauder slumped, then slipped from his mount. One foot caught in the stirrup so that his dead body bumped and leaped over the uneven ground. This broke the momentum of the attack. Another rider caught the dead man's horse, dismounted, and tossed their fallen comrade across his saddle. Abruptly, the group veered west toward the Bighorn Mountains.

The raid had been sudden and fast, but took a grim toll: two hands wounded, one seriously, and three horses dead or dying. The men carried the gut-shot hand into the house and the women tended to him while another hand, a rifle poking from his saddle scabbard, rode out to Widow Johnson's place on Sweetwater Creek. She was the closest thing to a doctor in the territory.

"Who in tarnal hell was it?" said Riley after the rest of the men had armed themselves and formed a perimeter guard in case of a second attempt.

Hanchon, staring at the dead claybank he had just put out of its misery, shook his head. Another hand had just quit on the spot and demanded his wages, claiming only a soft-brained fool would risk his life like this for beans and sowbelly. Hanchon knew he was right: This wasn't their fight.

"I didn't recognize any of 'em. But I'll wager Hiram Steele knows who they are."

"Steele's a rich man," said Riley. "And he's been selling remounts to the fort for a long time. I don't have much authority, but if he's behind this, I swear he *won't* get away with it."

"I expected trouble, but I never figured Steele had the stomach for this kind of business," said Hanchon bitterly. "He knows I can't go to law against him. The nearest U.S. marshal is in Laramie. That's two days' hard ride from here. 'Sides, what proof do I have?"

"The Army is the law out here," said Riley. "I'm going to my superiors about this. I'll take Corey as a witness."

Hanchon slowly nodded. "Give it a try, lad. But Steele is thick as thieves with that bunch at the fort. I got a feeling I'm in for six sorts of hell."

"The U. S. Army has no jurisdiction in civilian legal conflicts," said Lieutenant Seth Carlson. "We protect the settlers from Indians, yes, but *not* from each other."

Carlson was close to Tom Riley's age. But he held a permanent commission, and currently served as the adjutant to the commanding officer of the 7th Cavalry.

He was also, thought Corey, an arrogant, sneering bastard. Corey felt a warm glow of satisfaction as he recalled what Old Knobby at the feed stable in Bighorn Falls had told him—how Matthew had set the officer on his duff with two good punches.

"But sir—"

"Keep your 'buts' in your pocket, mister! You don't speak until I'm finished. I want to know why you took Kristen Steele out to the Hanchon spread with you?"

Riley's jaw slacked open in surprise at the unexpected question.

"We didn't take her. She came on her own, far as I could tell."

It was Carlson's turn to look surprised. He rose from behind his desk at Regimental Headquarters and paced nervously back and forth in front of a huge wall map of the Wyoming Territory. His hand rested on the hilt of his saber, nervously working it.

"She came on her own," he repeated woodenly, as if storing the fact away for later. Corey was not as baffled as Riley—he knew Carlson was trying to stake a claim to Kristen Steele. In fact, the jealous officer had jumped Matthew after learning about his secret visits to her.

"Yes, sir, on her own. But she's not the point here."

"Stow it, mister! The *point* is, from now on you best make sure she stays away from the Hanchon spread. Is that clear?"

"She's a civilian. What law says she can't visit where she's a mind to?"

"The same law that says my permanent silver bar outranks your temporary gold one. Is *that* clear?"

"Yes, sir."

Riley was visibly angry. But Corey realized he was also powerless.

"Are you saying," said Corey, "that you don't plan to do *nothing* about this?"

Carlson's lips curled in a sneer. "Clean the wax outta your ears, boy. That's exactly what I said."

"This ain't fair! John Hanchon done honest business with this fort for years."

"He *done* business with this fort," said Carlson, cutting him off. "You got that part right. But that's all behind us now."

Hot blood crept up the back of Corey's neck. "You got no right to let the Hanchons be drove out just on account of you had a fight with their boy Matthew."

"Stow it!"

"I ain't in no damn Army," said Corey. "You don't push me around."

But Riley gripped Corey's arm above the elbow, silencing him.

"Permission to leave, sir," he said to his superior.

Carlson glanced at Corey for a full ten seconds. "Dismissed," he finally said curtly.

Riley took two steps backwards, saluted smartly, then did an about-face and left, Corey in tow.

"We did what we could," said the young officer as Corey prepared to mount and leave the fort. "I'll keep my eyes peeled. But Hanchon was right as rain. There's no help to be had here."

Corey was silent for a long time, thinking. He knew that Matthew's tribe—Yellow Bear's Northern Cheyennes—had established their winter camp just north of the Bighorns halfway between the Powder and the Rosebud Rivers. But by now they would have returned to their summer camp at the fork where the Little Powder joined the Powder. It was perhaps three days' hard ride from here.

Corey slipped three fingers into the fob pocket of his vest, touching the specially notched and dyed blue feather which he always kept there. It had been given to him by Chief Yellow Bear himself after Corey had helped to save Yellow Bear's tribe from a Pawnee raid. It also guaranteed safe passage through Plains Indian country: Show it to any tribe, Yellow Bear explained, no matter if they were Sioux or Arapahoe or Shoshone, and they would treat him as a brave and honored friend of the red man.

Right there on the spot, Corey made up his mind.

"You're right," he said to Riley. "There's no help to be had here."

Corey knew Matthew was still his good friend, even though he was now called Touch the Sky and rejected the white man's ways. And he would never forgive him if Corey sat idly by while Matthew's adopted parents were ruined and driven out—maybe even killed.

Soon all hell's gonna be a-poppin', thought Corey. *But tomorrow I ride north into Cheyenne country.*

Chapter Two

Touch the Sky lifted aside the elkskin flap covering the entrance to his tipi and stepped out into the cool morning mist.

His sister the sun was just beginning her journey across the sky. The short white days of the cold moons were over. It was now the Moon When the Green Grass Is Up, and the Cheyenne pony herds had been turned loose from their rope corrals to graze in the lush meadows bordering the Powder River.

Touch the Sky had 17 winters behind him. The young Cheyenne was lean and straight and tall, with a strong hawk nose and keen black eyes. His black hair hung in loose locks except where it had been cropped close above his brows to keep his vision clear. He wore beaded leggings, a breechclout of soft kid leather, elkskin moccasins.

He paused outside his tipi and listened to the strong, deep voice of an old squaw as she sang the Song to the Sun Rising. Then he glanced across the camp clearing toward a lone tipi reigning by itself on a low hummock between the river and the rest of camp: Chief Yellow Bear's tipi.

White plumes curled from the smokehole at the top. But Touch the Sky knew it was not smoke from a cooking fire. The old chief lay near death. Now the tribal medicine man, Arrow Keeper, kept incense burning day and night while members of the tribe took turns sitting beside the chief's sleeping robes, singing the ancient cure songs.

Most of the tipis were erected in circles by clans. The center of camp was reserved for the council lodge—a huge willow-branch frame covered with buffalo hides. In front of the council lodge, a pole had been carved with the magic totems of the tribe. The enemy scalps dangling from it looked like tufts of coarse hair clipped from horse tails.

A cooking fire blazed in front of Arrow Keeper's tipi. Touch the Sky felt his stomach churning in hunger when he smelled elk steaks sizzling over the tripod. He had started to cross the clearing toward Arrow Keeper's tipi when a mocking voice behind him stopped Touch the Sky in his tracks.

"Woman Face!"

Angry blood pulsing in his temples, he turned to face the speaker.

"You are walking in the wrong direction," said Wolf Who Hunts Smiling. "The women's sewing lodge is at the other end of camp."

The speaker had a wily face befitting his name, with swift, furtive eyes that missed nothing. Wolf

Who Hunts Smiling had been present when Bluecoat pony soldiers killed his father. Now he despised all whites with a hatred unmatched by anyone else in the tribe. He had accused Touch the Sky of being a spy for the whites ever since the wandering outcast had been captured still wearing his white man's clothing. The mocking name "Woman Face" was a reference to Touch the Sky's former habit of letting his emotions show in his face—a white man's habit despised by Cheyennes as unmanly.

Touch the Sky saw Wolf Who Hunts Smiling carefully eye the knife in his sheath. The obsidian blade was small but honed on one side to a lethal edge that could shave the callus off a pony's hoof.

"Call me Woman Face again," said Touch the Sky, his features stony, "and you will humiliate your clan when this *woman* feeds your liver to the dogs."

Wolf Who Hunts Smiling was accompanied by another of Touch the Sky's sworn enemies in the tribe, Swift Canoe of the Wolverine Clan. Swift Canoe blamed him for the death of his twin brother, True Son, during a raid against the lice-eating Pawnees. But Touch the Sky alone knew it was Wolf Who Hunts Smiling's disobedience which had alerted the Pawnees and resulted in True Son's death.

Both of his enemies stared at him, their eyes revealing the hatred their faces refused to show. But wisely, neither of them tested his boast. They had witnessed his courage under torture and strength in battle.

"He talks the he-bear talk now," said Wolf Who Hunts Smiling. "He knows he is safe here in the middle of camp. Perhaps he has forgotten that I have walked between him and the fire."

"I have not forgotten this thing," said Touch the Sky. "What? Forgotten it? I am weary of hearing you repeat it like the camp crier. Words are nothing, things of smoke. Let your battle axe speak for you. For my part, I have no desire to kill either of you. Have you listened to the counsel of Arrow Keeper and Yellow Bear and the elders? We have enough enemies. It is foolish to kill each other."

For a moment, his unexpected words softened the hatred in the eyes of his enemies. Then, perhaps recalling the sight as Bluecoat canister shot turned his unarmed father into stewmeat, Wolf Who Hunts Smiling said bitterly, "A dog who sleeps in manure stinks like manure. You may dress like a Cheyenne, talk like a Cheyenne. But you have the white man's stink on you for life!"

Touch the Sky abruptly turned his back on both of them and joined Arrow Keeper. The old shaman had squatted near the tripod to collect the tasty fat dripping from the steaks, catching it on a broad leaf.

"Good morning, Father. How is Yellow Bear?" the youth greeted him. Wolf Who Hunts Smiling's parting remark had left angry veins pulsing over his temples. Perhaps it was true and Touch the Sky didn't have the courage to accept it. Perhaps he *did* have the white man's stink all over him.

Arrow Keeper, whose medicine bundle was the owl, drew his blanket around him tighter and slowly shook his head. The old medicine man's long gray hair was shot through with parched white streaks. His ancient face was still hatchet-sharp in profile, but as wrinkled as an old apple core.

He made the cut-off sign in answer to Touch the Sky's question. It was bad luck to use the word death directly.

"He will soon be called to the Land of Ghosts. I fear greatly for the tribe. The loss of a chief is strong bad medicine for his people. Our enemies, hearing of it, may well choose such a time to attack."

These words troubled Touch the Sky. He had already witnessed the awful death and destruction Pawnees had inflicted in a surprise raid on Yellow Bear's tribe.

Arrow Keeper read these thoughts in the young buck's troubled eyes. It was the old shaman's important mission to protect the tribe's four sacred Medicine Arrows with his very life. The fate of the arrows, always kept clean in their coyote fur pouch, was the fate of the tribe. If the Medicine Arrows were lost, the tribe was lost.

"Yellow Bear has served his ten winters as chief," said Touch the Sky. "Cannot the Headmen appoint a new leader?"

Arrow Keeper shook his bead. "The chief-renewal ceremony should be held now that the snows have melted. But the Sun Dance, and the required feasting, cannot take place while our chief lies ill."

Touch the Sky glanced again toward Yellow Bear's tipi. "And Honey Eater? How is she?"

Worry smoldered deep in Arrow Keeper's dark eyes as he thought about Yellow Bear's daughter. "She is like a beautiful lark that has forgotten how to sing. Her father's death will leave her alone. You must be strong. She loves you straight and true, little brother. But as you know well,

Black Elk has already sent her the gift of horses. True, she returned them. But her father was well then. The Cheyenne way will not permit her to remain unmarried for long once her father leaves this world."

Touch the Sky nodded, deeply troubled. Only a battle-tested warrior could court and undergo the squaw-taking ceremony. He was now a blooded warrior. And Honey Eater had declared her love for him. But besides two fine ponies, what riches could he bring to the marriage? And her refusal of Black Elk's bride-price had led that fiercely jealous young war chief to declare to Touch the Sky: *Know this. There must come a time when Honey Eater either accepts my horses or you and I must fight to the death!*

Touch the Sky saw the entrance flap of Yellow Bear's tipi lifted aside; then Honey Eater stepped outside.

She was distracted with worry and did not notice him. Again Touch the Sky admired the frail beauty of her high, finely sculpted cheekbones. Her long black hair was braided with white petals of mountain columbine. Her buckskin dress was ornamented with elk teeth and eagle tails, with gold coins serving as buttons.

She joined a group of girls who were headed toward the women's lodge. Some were already, as they walked, stripping bark from willow stems with their teeth. They would use the stems to weave baskets for gathering berries, which would be dried and stored for the cold moons.

Suddenly, the camp crier burst into view over the rise south of camp. "The hunting party has returned early!" he shouted, riding up and down through the village. "Firetop rides with them!"

Immediately, excited voices buzzed throughout the camp. Touch the Sky couldn't believe his ears. Firetop was the name the tribe had bestowed upon his friend Corey Robinson when they honored the redhead as a savior of the tribe. He had faced down great danger when, pretending to be insane, he had frightened the superstitious Pawnees away before they could launch their bloody second raid on Yellow Bear's camp.

Now the hunting party, led by a young brave named River of Winds, topped the rise. By now the central camp clearing was crowded with braves, elders wrapped in their bright Hudson's Bay blankets, naked children dashing around like the excited dogs. When the redhead broke into view on his big blood gelding, a warrior honored him by raising the Cheyenne war cry.

"Hiya hi-i-i-ya!"

It was repeated by all the warriors, Touch the Sky included. By the time the party reached the clan circles, Corey's horse was forced to a standstill by the knot of Cheyennes trying to touch and greet him. Corey smiled sheepishly as hands groped for him, squaws attempted to hand him food, gifts were showered on him.

Finally Touch the Sky worked his way closer and Corey spotted him. His gap-toothed grin widened.

"Matthew!" he shouted, offering his hand from force of habit. Then, quickly, he withdrew it, remembering that his friend could no longer follow the white man's customs.

"Touch the Sky!" he corrected himself. "God-in-whirlwinds, am I glad to see you!"

Momentarily moved at seeing his good friend again, Touch the Sky permitted himself a rare smile. But the English words felt stiff and heavy in his mouth when he said, "Good to see you too, Corey."

Despite his joy, Touch the Sky was worried. He knew that Corey would not have made the long, dangerous ride across Plains Indian country just to pay a social call. His special blue feather was no protection from enemies of the Cheyenne. But it was almost mid-morning before the two friends finally found themselves alone in Touch the Sky's tipi.

" 'Fraid I got bad news," Corey said bluntly as soon as they had settled in among the elkskins and buffalo robes.

Carefully, leaving nothing out, he told all of it: how Hiram Steele had driven the Hanchons out of the mercantile business; how someone, most likely Steele, had harassed the Hanchons all winter, attacking hands and killing horses and even trying to burn the homesteaders out; how Seth Carlson and his superiors at the fort were deliberately ignoring the dangerous situation.

Touch the Sky struggled to keep the emotions from his face as Corey spoke. But anger at Steele boiled up inside him like a tight bubble escaping. It was tempered only by fear and concern for the only parents he had ever known—good, loving parents who had bucked all criticism by raising a Cheyenne boy among whites. After all, it was to protect them that he had left in the first place.

"Come with me," said Touch the Sky when Corey was finished.

The two youths sought out old Arrow Keeper at his tipi. Touch the Sky explained everything Corey had told him. When he was finished, he said, "Father, what should I do? I am a Shaiyena.

But these two whites are the soul of my medicine bag. How can I let these things happen to them? Am I not a warrior? Is their battle not mine?"

Arrow Keeper was silent a long time, his seamed face impassive.

"Only three sleeps ago I had a troubling medicine dream," he said finally, almost to himself. "This thing was foretold."

Now he looked at the young Cheyenne.

"Do you realize what the rest will think and say if you desert your tribe now? Now, when your chief will soon rest on his burial scaffold and leave the tribe vulnerable to attack?"

Unable to keep all the misery from showing in his face, Touch the Sky nodded.

"And, little brother, have you also considered Honey Eater? She loves you. But Black Elk loves her. When Yellow Bear leaves us—and soon he must—she will need you more than ever. She will be alone. A Cheyenne who is alone is a dead Cheyenne. Do you have ears for my meaning?"

Again Touch the Sky nodded. His heart felt heavy as a stone. Arrow Keeper was telling him that she would almost surely have to marry Black Elk if Touch the Sky were gone too long.

"Tell me," said the old shaman, "do you love these white people? Were they good to you?"

Touch the Sky nodded. "They were good to me. I would die for them as I would for the tribe."

Another long silence. Then Arrow Keeper repeated to himself, "It was all foretold."

He seemed to reach some decision. He met the young Cheyenne's eyes.

"Place these words in your sash and carry them with you always. Your place is with your tribe. You know I speak only one way, straight-arrow.

My heart is a stone toward most whites. But some there are"—here he looked at Corey with fondness in his red-rimmed eyes—"who are friends to the red man. A Cheyenne who forsakes his father and mother, no matter what color their skin, is no Cheyenne."

His last words surprised Touch the Sky.

"You are a blooded warrior now," Arrow Keeper said. "I have spoken. Now let your heart decide. I have seen the mark of the warrior buried in your hair, and I have spoken to you of the great vision I experienced at Medicine Lake. It told me that a great destiny is in store for you as a war chief of the Cheyennes. I trust in this medicine dream, though indeed, it may have been a false vision placed over my eyes by enemy magic.

"Now make your decision, Cheyenne brave. Do you go to help these whites who raised you, knowing it may turn your tribe against you forever and cost you Honey Eater? Or do you stay?"

It felt like a hot knife was being twisted deep in his guts. But Touch the Sky's mouth was a determined slit—he knew what he had to do.

"I go to my parents. Their battle is my battle."

Old Arrow Keeper held his face impassive. But a brief twinkle in his eyes told the youth that he was proud of this decision.

"Then go," he said simply, turning his back in dismissal.

Chapter Three

"No need to get ice in your boots," said Hiram Steele. "Hanchon can't prove nothing. You just keep following the plan, and I'll make you a rich man."

Seth Carlson was impatient to broach the subject of Kristen's visits to the Hanchon spread. But Steele got blood in his eyes quick when anyone pushed into his personal life.

"I ain't getting icy boots," Carlson said. "I'm just telling you, he's filed a homestead at the Territorial Office. He aims to prove up the land and stay."

"Where you been grazing? That's old news. Well, maybe he filed a homestead, but I'll wager he won't be roosting there. John Hanchon's got no spine for fighting."

Steele was a big, heavy-jowled, flint-eyed man in homespun shirt and trousers and a rawhide vest. He stood in front of a fieldstone fireplace in the parlor of his spacious, notched-log house. The room's sole reminder of his dead wife was a cherry spinet against the back wall. Bearskin rugs were scattered across the plank floor.

" 'Pears to me," said the young lieutenant, "he's got more starch in his collar than you credit him with. He stood up to that raid good enough last Sunday."

"He's small potatoes," insisted Steele. "Besides, it takes plenty of help to run a mustang spread. Even if Hanchon does have enough sand in him to stick it out, it's getting hard for him to feed and pay help. Ain't too many men want to put their bacon in the fire for three hots and a cot. This new bunch I hired on, they ain't wranglers. These are hard-bitten men who'd rather risk getting shot to doing honest work. One man killed won't stop them."

"That shines right," agreed Carlson. "But Tom Riley worries me. He's thick with the Hanchons and that freckle-faced sprout that was friends with their Injun boy."

"Has this Riley got friends at the fort?"

"Nobody that counts. But he can be muleheaded and he's often on maneuvers with the new recruits. He could easy poke around enough to find out it's your men that's been raiding the Hanchon spread."

Steele shrugged. "Then let him. Finding out something ain't the same as proving it. Just keep an eye on him. He starts causing us any trouble, we'll make him regret it. Won't be the first green officer that got knocked out from under his hat by a bullet out here on the frontier."

Carlson sensed that the moment was right to

bring up the topic he was aching to mention.

"And I'm just the man to do it," he said. "I don't like the way he looks at Kristen."

Steele's brows rose at the mention of his daughter. "Kristen? Where the hell does he know her from?"

"Why, from the Hanchons, I reckon."

"The Hanchons? She's got orders from me to have nothing to do with them. I made sure of that when I drove their redskin buck off."

Carlson's habitual sneer twisted into a frown. "I was just coming to that. It's none of my mix, you being her father and all. But I was going to mention to you that she shouldn't be visiting their spread. She was out there when your men raided."

Steele's eyes turned smoky with rage. His voice was dangerously quiet when he said, "She was out there? You know that?"

"Riley and the Robinson boy both told me. Besides being dangerous for her, it doesn't look good for me. Career officers don't hitch up with women who hobnob with Injun lovers. Not if they want to keep their commission."

Carlson didn't bother to add the fact that much of the resentment smoldering in his words now was because of the sound thrashing Matthew Hanchon had given him a year ago—when Carlson had threatened to ruin Hanchon's contract with Fort Bates if the Cheyenne didn't clear out for good.

"You say you got your C.O. believing there's Injun trouble?"

Carlson nodded.

"I'm thinking," said Steele, "that the U.S. Army ought to maybe post a sentry, just as a courtesy to the Hanchons. Maybe on top Thompson's Bluff."

Carlson thought about it and nodded again. "I could authorize that on my own." He knew full well that Steele too had Kristen in mind, not renegade Indians.

Steele paced once around the room, his hob-nail boots echoing on the planks. Then, without a word, he went out front of the house and banged the triangle three times—the signal for summoning Kristen to the house.

She was daydreaming in a sheltered copse south of the house when Kristen heard her father's signal. For a moment she was tempted to pretend she hadn't heard it. The morning's chores were finished and she just wanted to go on listening to the sweet song of the meadowlarks, to the angry jay scolding her from a coarse-barked cottonwood nearby.

But reluctantly she decided to obey her father's summons. Slowly she emerged from the copse, the secret spot where she and Matthew used to meet. At the same moment, she watched a doe with a fawn break from a thicket down near the river. It had been a hard winter in the high country, and deer had come down into the lower valleys to escape the snow. How, she wondered, had the winter been for Matthew? Was he even still alive?

She was halfway back to the house when she saw a quick-darting prairie falcon swoop down on an unsuspecting squirrel. Kristen shivered when the squirrel suddenly chittered in fright that quickly turned to pain. It made her again recall that awful day when her father and the hired hand Boone Wilson had likewise pounced on her and Matthew in the copse. Never would she forget how she had been forced to lie to save Matthew's life—how she had looked him right in the eye and told him she never wanted to see him again. Something had died inside of him on that day; soon after, he had left to join the Cheyenne Indians.

Corey had told her a little bit about Matthew's new life since then. And though Corey had said nothing about what happened to Boone Wilson, she couldn't help wondering—could it have been Matthew who left the bullying, murderous Indian-hater dead and scalped in the road?

As she neared the house, she noted a hired hand repairing the broken tongue of a wagon. Another was splitting stove lengths with a wedge; still others worked green horses in the pole corral. Her gentle piebald, too lazy to require picketing, drank from the rain barrel at one corner of the house. There was nothing out of the ordinary to explain her father's summons.

Again, for a moment, she thought of the new men her father had recently hired. These were not the usual types who showed up willing to "earn their breakfast," as her father put it. They were mean, dirty, lazy men who looked out at the world from lidded eyes and surly faces. What good were they on a mustang spread?

Then she lost that thought when she spotted Seth Carlson's handsome cavalry black, reins looped over the tie-rail. Her pulse quickened in nervous anticipation.

A moment later the officer himself emerged from the house and mounted.

Kristen ducked behind the corner of an outbuilding so he wouldn't spot her. Ever since Matthew had been run off, Carlson had been coming around more and more. Why he spent so much time secretly conferring with her father, she didn't know. But the arrogant young officer had made it clear he wanted to marry her. Kristen had already decided she would run away before she would let that happen.

She lifted the latch string and opened the door. A moment later she cried out in surprise and pain as her father met her at the door with a vicious slap to the face.

"The hell you mean by defying me, girl?"

The stinging blow left her ears ringing and brought tears leaping to her eyelashes. "What do you mean?"

Another hard slap left her dizzy. Moments later he had her pressed against the back of the door, her arms pinioned.

"Don't play the larks with me, girl, I'm warning you! I'm talking about you sneaking around behind my back to visit the Hanchons."

"I only wanted to see their new place."

"I don't care *what* you wanted! I won't brook defiance, you hear me?"

"But Father! I—"

She cried out in fright when he snarled like a rabid animal and threw her hard to the floor.

"Shut your cake-hole, girl, and listen to me! Don't have *nothing* more to do with the Hanchons or their redskin boy. No daughter of mine gives the time of day to Injun-lovers. You hear me?"

He towered over her, frightening in his rage. Kristen wanted to tell him he was all wrong about the Hanchons and Matthew. She wanted to tell him that this was wrong, unfair. But she knew protest was useless. When he was in a rage like this, all she could do was humor him.

"Yes, Father."

"I mean it. You don't have anything more to do with any of that bunch. It's bad enough my men saw my own daughter kissing that redskin pup of theirs. Your mother and I raised you decent."

Kristen wished she had the courage to ask if his "decency" had included that Sunday raid on the Hanchon spread. But wisely, she bit back her retort.

"Yes, Father," she repeated. But suddenly, even as she spoke, Kristen knew she would have to defy her father. For one thing, she would have to warn the Hanchons. Whatever Seth Carlson and her father were up to, it meant that John and Sarah Hanchon were in for a world of grief.

And, if he was foolish enough to return again, so was Matthew.

At 0700 hours sharp, Brevet Officer Tom Riley conducted morning roll call and inspection of his platoon of new recruits. His hat in one hand, he was about to knock smartly on the door of the Regimental Headquarters Office to make his morning report.

The door was not quite closed. He hesitated, recognizing the voice which easily carried through the one-inch gap between the jamb and the door. Seth Carlson.

"We have evidence, sir, that it was renegade Cheyennes who attacked the Hanchon spread. They first robbed a mining camp near the Crazy Woman Fork of the Sweetwater, stealing white men's clothing, weapons, and shod horses. Then they attacked the Hanchons dressed as white men, apparently planning to steal horses."

Riley's jaw dropped open in astonishment. He

leaned closer and pressed one eye to the gap.

"Renegade Cheyennes?" said Major Bruce Harding, regimental commander. "According to the last scouting report, all the Cheyennes in the territory are camped up near the Powder."

"Yes, sir, they were. But we think this is a small band of warriors in the Dog Soldier Society. That's one of the Cheyennes' military societies, led by a younger warrior who's rebelled against their peace leader."

Riley watched Major Harding lean back in his chair. He was a small, neat, worried-looking man who constantly rubbed one knuckle across his mustache, smoothing it. He did so now as he stared at the huge territorial map covering one wall.

"How do you know," said Harding, "that the redskins who robbed the miners also attacked the Hanchons?"

"One of the Injuns was shot and dropped his rifle. It was an old Kentucky over-and-under, carved with the initials of one of the miners."

Riley couldn't believe his ears! Carlson had shown absolutely no interest in investigating the attack when he and Corey reported it. Now he was making up a pack of lies about it. Carlson knew damn good and well that the Cheyenne Dog Soldier Society had not been active anywhere north of the Platte River for at least two years. But he also knew that Harding was ignorant and incompetent, a West Point graduate who had never commanded a garrison before Fort Bates.

Riley, his face flushing warm with angry blood, was about to push the door open and storm into the C.O.'s office.

Then he realized: If he did that, Carlson would

know that someone had spotted his hand before he played it. *Why warn him now,* thought Riley, *when I can wait and see exactly what he's up to?* Besides, Major Harding was a staunch Indian-hater. Why should he believe a temporary recruit-platoon commander over his own adjutant?

"I expected this kind of trouble," said Harding. "I say the government must either fish or cut bait. Either give this damn territory to the savages, and make sure they *stay* here, or take it for the white man. But Washington and the Indian-lovers in Congress have tied my hands. We are technically at peace with the red nations, so any type of organized offensive campaign is out of the question."

"Yes, sir," said Carlson. "But we are authorized to mount small troop movements. It might be a good idea to keep Tom Riley's trainees camped further north of here, closer to the Indian hunting grounds. That way they can observe the Cheyennes and establish a military presence as a reminder. We can also step up patrols closer to the fort."

Harding, smoothing his mustache, approved this with a nod. "This new trouble will also put some teeth into my request to Washington for more troops."

Harding thought of something else. "If we step up patrols, we'll need more remounts. Can Steele provide them?"

Carlson nodded. "Yes, sir. I spoke with him recently, and he informed me that he has a corral full of fresh-broke mustangs. Top-notch horseflesh."

So that's *the gait,* thought Riley. Carlson and Steele were feeding at the same trough! That explained the "Indian menace." This way, Carlson got Riley out of the picture so Steele's men could freely raid the Hanchon spread. And not only did that story allow Steele to secretly ruin John Hanchon. False reports about "Indian scares" were common because they stirred up settlers. Stirred-up settlers meant more soldiers, and thus, more lucrative contracts to opportunists like Steele for supplying them. Major Harding was perfect for their scheme. He considered Indians heathens without morality, an obstacle to Puritan progress.

Besides, Harding had a brother in the St. Louis settlements, a master gunsmith who was making a small fortune by arming the spirit of Westward expansion.

Riley made up his mind right then and there—he was sending a letter by guardmail to the territorial commander at Fort Laramie. The lieutenant colonel in charge of that garrison had a reputation, scorned by many of his fellow soldiers, for negotiating with red men rather than simply hunting them down.

"Sir," said Carlson, "I agree that we should either fish or cut bait. It won't do much good to increase patrols if the men are still restricted from returning fire."

His meaning was clear to Harding. The C.O. debated for a long moment, one knuckle worrying his mustache.

"As a purely practical matter," said Harding, "it's safe to assume that any Cheyennes caught in this area are up to no good, right?"

Carlson nodded. "They're either killing or thieving, sir. There's no other reason for them to be this far south."

Harding nodded again. Then he said, "Send the company clerk in when you leave, Lieutenant. Until these attacks subside, I'm authorizing an emergency shoot-to-kill order against the Cheyenne tribe."

Chapter Four

At last the tall grass finally gave way to the shortgrass prairie. Now Touch the Sky and Corey turned due south toward the Tongue River valley and the river-bend settlement of Bighorn Falls.

Touch the Sky had left two magnificent ponies back with the Cheyenne herds—a beautiful spotted gray, the prize for counting first coup on a Crow brave, and a swift, powerful cavalry sorrel. This last was his by right of killing the white whiskey trader, Henri Lagace, in fair combat. But Touch the Sky was saving both of these ponies as part of the bride-price he hoped to offer for Honey Eater. Instead, he now rode the pony he trusted most, the spirited dun Arrow Keeper had given him.

They avoided wagon tracks and the new forts with their loopholed gun towers and squared-off walls of cottonwood logs. Only the discipline of a blooded warrior kept Touch the Sky from thinking of this familiar route as a journey "home"—home to big trouble with his old enemy Hiram Steele. Nor did he allow himself to worry about what they must be saying about him back at Yellow Bear's camp.

Instead, he obeyed the teachings of Arrow Keeper and Black Elk. He tried to keep his mind free of any worry or thoughts except awareness of the present. He kept his attention focused on the helpful language of nature.

Thus, he immediately worried about it when a startled sparrowhawk suddenly flew off from a tangled deadfall well ahead, where the sloping wall of the valley crowded the game trail they were following.

Touch the Sky gave the high sign to Corey, halting him. The young Cheyenne only needed to pat his pony's neck once and she stopped—already troubled by whatever sense of danger had alerted Touch the Sky. She laid her ears back, snorting something to Corey's big gelding.

Touch the Sky warned Corey with his eyes not to move. Then he slid to the ground silently and hobbled his pony. Unsheathing his obsidian knife, he clutched it at the ready in his teeth. He had recently fashioned a strong new bow from oak and shaped and feathered a quiverful of arrows. He slid one of the arrows out and strung it. The shaft was made from dead pine, the point hardened in fire.

His moccasined feet moved silently as he neared the deadfall. His heart throbbed in his palms, but he concentrated, watching for the slightest movement.

His arm drew the arrow back a few inches, tightening the buffalo-sinew bowstring.

A few heartbeats later, the sharp stone tip of a streamered lance thrust forth out of the deadfall and stopped just short of skewering the hollow of his throat.

"You just died without singing the death song, careless Cheyenne warrior!"

Recognizing the voice before he saw a face, Touch the Sky lowered his bow and took the knife from his teeth so he could speak.

"Little Horse!"

His friend, permitting himself a grin of triumph, emerged from the tangle of brush.

"Good thing for you and Firetop I only counted coup, brother. If I were a lice-eating Pawnee, your scalps would be dangling from my clout."

"Good thing that few lice-eaters strike as silently as you. But what are you doing this far from camp?"

Little Horse was small but his compact body was powerful and sure in its movements. Like Touch the Sky he wore a leather band around his left wrist for protection from the slap of his bowstring. He circled around behind the deadfall and retrieved his pony.

"I am going with you and Firetop," he said. "I asked Arrow Keeper why you rode off. He explained this thing with your white parents. I told him you and Firetop should not face these paleface dogs alone. He agreed and gave me permission to join you. I caught up with you this morning, then passed you by riding hard above the rim of the valley."

"You have already saved my life once from white dogs. This is my battle and you owe me nothing. Ride back to our people, brother."

Little Horse stubbornly shook his head. "True it is, I saved your life in the paleface camp. But who saved Honey Eater from them? Who stood up to a night of torture that would have killed or broken a lesser brave? Who courageously sang the death song and prepared to ram an arrow down his own throat rather than help an enemy? And when the scar-face who sold devil water and slaughtered our people escaped, who trailed him across the plains and killed him?

"You are a true Cheyenne warrior, and your medicine is strong! We are brothers. Our blood is one. Therefore, our battles are one. And if we fall, we will fall as one. Not on the ground, brother, but on the bones of our enemies!"

A tight lump rose in Touch the Sky's throat, and he was silent for a long moment. He knew well that Little Horse was paying dearly for this loyalty. Even with Arrow Keeper's blessing, the Headmen would be furious that a strong young buck, a blooded warrior and one of Black Elk's favorites, had left the tribe to fight a battle for whites.

"Then let us ride," said Touch the Sky. He knew it would insult Little Horse to thank him more directly. "We are still two full sleeps from our destination."

Corey, who knew only a few words in Cheyenne, said, "What did Little Horse and you talk about?"

"Little Horse is fighting beside us against Steele."

They rode hard for the rest of that day, subsisting on cold river water and the dried venison the Cheyennes carried in their legging sashes. Several times they dismounted at game trails to search for moccasin prints. They were relieved that there was no sign of the distinctive cross-weave stitching of the Pawnees.

Besides the Bluecoats, the many enemies of the Cheyennes and their nearby cousins, the Lakota Sioux, included the Absaraka or Crow tribe and the turncoat Utes who lived in the high country. But among their Indian enemies, all Cheyennes most feared and hated the bloodthirsty Pawnees.

Nearly thirty winters ago, Pawnees had captured the Cheyennes' sacred Medicine Arrows. Though the Cheyennes had gotten them back in a revenge strike, the two tribes had been mortal enemies ever since. The lice-eaters had proven themselves eager mercenaries for the strong water and trinkets of the long knives, razing many Indian villages for them. The fierce Lakotas had at one time driven all Pawnees from the Powder River country. But they had begun drifting back. And Touch the Sky feared they would again attack Yellow Bear's camp—while warriors were in short supply and he and Little Horse were gone.

On the first night after Little Horse joined them, the trio slept in a cold camp near the game trail. Touch the Sky had spotted a spruce grove near a good patch of graze. They tethered their horses with long strips of rawhide. Then they pushed the drooping spruce branches aside and disappeared inside. They spread their robes on the deep mat of needles and slept in a hidden lodge of silence, safe from all eyes.

"Brother," whispered Little Horse after Corey's deep, even breathing signaled that he was asleep. "I would speak with you."

"I have ears for your words. Speak them."

Little Horse waited for a moment, listening to make sure Corey was still asleep.

"I mean no disrespect toward Firetop," Little Horse assured him. "His medicine is strong, and by right of courage he is one of us. But we will soon be among other whites. I must ask that you not say my name in front of them. Introduce me as War Eagle, but avoid even that false name."

It wasn't necessary to explain his meaning. Indians believed their names lost power if spoken by other Indians in front of whites.

Touch the Sky had learned this from Arrow Keeper but forgotten. Now he thought about it, then nodded.

"Of course, brother. In front of whites, I will not call you by any name but brother."

"Nor I you. Do not be offended. I will honor your parents as my own."

On the second night they sheltered in an old bear den in the cliffs overlooking the Tongue River. Earlier that day they had killed a deer and butchered out the loin and kidneys. Now, safe within the well-hidden den, they built a small cooking fire to roast the meat.

Later, before he drifted off in bone-weary sleep, Touch the Sky heard the ferocious kill-cry of a badger. It shot chills through him, reminding him of the Cheyenne's own shrill war cry—and reminding him that death and danger lurked nearby constantly on the frontier. Nor was it only animals and red men who must fight constantly for survival. Were his white parents not locked in a struggle for their very existence? Black Elk was a harsh man tempered more by battle than by love.

But he was right. Life meant always being a warrior.

And perhaps, after all, that kill-cry had been an omen: The next morning they rode into trouble.

They were making the most dangerous leg of the journey, crossing the vast, open stretch of sage flats surrounding Bighorn Falls. It was a level range pockmarked by prairie-dog towns, making footing dangerous for the tired ponies. Halfway across the flats, their path crossed that of a squad of Bluecoat pony soldiers from the soldiertown of Fort Bates.

The three held a hasty council as the squad drew closer. Touch the Sky translated when necessary.

"We should try to outrun them," said Little Horse.

"I think not, brother," said Touch the Sky. "I know it is foolish to trust Bluecoats. But our ponies are tired, and truly, where would we run? Recall that talking papers have been signed, papers which say there is no war between red men and white."

Little Horse considered these things, then nodded. "The talking papers are nothing. The white man speaks two ways always. Still, I have ears for your words. We are with Firetop. Surely they will not fire upon a white man."

Touch the Sky repeated all this for Corey.

"Sure, Little Horse is using his head! I ain't heard of no trouble lately between Indians and the cavalry at Fort Bates. Besides, plenty of the soldiers know me. It might even be Tom Riley, though that's not his paint this officer is riding. If they challenge us, I'll tell 'em I got lost around the upcountry of the river and you two brung me back on account of my blue feather requiring you to."

Touch the Sky explained this plan to Little Horse and he nodded his approval. They rode on, the two Cheyennes folding their arms in the symbol of peace.

"What in tarnal hell?" said Corey nervously when, still several hundred yards away, the squad suddenly formed into a skirmish line. The officer leading them raised his saber, then lowered it sharply in the signal to attack.

"Ride like the wind!" shouted Touch the Sky to Little Horse in Cheyenne. To Corey he said, "You just stay here! If you don't run, they won't hurt you. It's us they plan to kill!"

"Then, by God, they'll have to kill three of us! Gee-up!" Corey urged his mount.

A moment later, startling both of his companions, Corey unleashed a ferocious Cheyenne battle cry: *"Hiya hi-i-i-ya!"*

The trio drove their exhausted mounts mercilessly, racing far too quickly across the uneven, pockmarked terrain. Their destination was the river valley with its protective thickets. But Touch the Sky knew they'd never reach it in time. Already the first bullets were whining past their ears, raising dust plumes all around them.

The two Cheyennes instinctively flattened themselves low against their ponies' necks to make a smaller target. Corey made do with hunkering low over the saddle horn. They had only one firearm between them, the old breechloader protruding from Corey's saddle scabbard. He pulled it out and laid it across the saddle at the ready. Touch the Sky and Little Horse, having practiced this so many times the movements came without thought, strung their bows at a full gallop.

"Brother!" shouted Touch the Sky to Little Horse above the hollow thunder of their horses' hooves. "They are closing too quickly! Remember what Black Elk taught us. When all seems lost, we must turn the fox into the rabbit!"

Little Horse nodded, understanding that it was their only chance. It was an ancient Cheyenne fighting trick to split up during a retreat and divide the enemy force. A brave would then suddenly turn in mid-flight and attack his surprised enemy.

The two Cheyennes veered sharply to either flank while Corey continued straight toward the river valley. As Touch the Sky had hoped, the pony soldiers ignored the white youth and divided up to pursue him and Little Horse.

One of the Bluecoats, a young corporal on a powerful bay, surged ahead of the others pursuing Touch the Sky. The Cheyenne waited until the NCO had closed to within perhaps 50 yards. Abruptly, Touch the Sky jerked back hard on the dun's buffalo-hair bridle. The battle-trained pony responded magnificently, whirling to reverse herself seemingly without breaking stride.

The corporal's jaw dropped in astonished disbelief when he realized he was suddenly under attack. In a heartbeat Touch the Sky was upon him, streamered battle lance pointing before him. His eyes met the soldier's, and he saw that his enemy was barely older than he was. He read fear in those eyes, but also the determination to fight and die like a man.

At the last moment Touch the Sky diverted his lance, cracking it down harmlessly on the bay's hindquarters.

"I have counted first coup, Bluecoat!" he shouted in English as both of them halted and turned their mounts. "I would let you live, that forever you will speak of Cheyenne bravery! Now make your choice."

The soldier started to lift his carbine. Then he lowered it. His face showed confusion at this spectacle of an English-speaking Indian who had just spared his life.

"I'll be damned if my weapon didn't just hangfire on me!" he said. "But get the hell clear of here *now* and stay out! We got orders to shoot all Cheyennes on sight!"

Touch the Sky had already touched heels to his pony. He was just in time to watch Little Horse turn on his surprised pursuer. The Bluecoat got off just one shot, missing the brave, before Little Horse knocked him from the saddle with a deft sideways sweep of his lance.

But now the officer leading the charge on his powerful black was bearing down on Touch the Sky, saber raised for the kill. Again Touch the Sky whirled around to face the attack, an arrow strung in his bow.

When the officer had closed to about 20 yards, Touch the Sky recognized Lieutenant Seth Carlson.

For a long moment their eyes held in mutual recognition and hatred. Then, as quick as a blink, one of the black's forelegs sank deep into a prairie-dog hole. The bone snapped with a loud sound like green wood splitting. Carlson flew head over heels from the saddle and hit the ground hard.

At the sound of the injured horse's scream of pain, another cavalry mount balked, snorting bloody foam. With two men down, including their badly shaken lieutenant, the momentum of the charge was broken.

There was no one in pursuit as Touch the Sky and Little Horse raced to join Corey. But even as he felt the swelling elation of victory, Touch the Sky recalled the hatred smoldering in Carlson's eyes. And again he heard the corporal's ominous warning: *We got orders to shoot all Cheyennes on sight!*

Chapter Five

"I shan't stay long, Mrs. Hanchon," said Kristen. "Pa will skin me alive if he finds out I've been here again since that trouble last Sunday. He thinks I'm at Holly Miller's house in town, being fit for a dress."

The two women were walking back from the small, windowless shed John Hanchon had constructed over a spring to keep food cold. Kristen wore a split buckskin skirt and a leather jerkin. She and Sarah had met before they reached the yard. Now Kristen led her lazy piebald by the reins. Sarah carried a wooden pail of milk.

Sarah halted and used her free hand to sweep the golden curls away from Kristen's left cheek. There were still faint, puffy blue traces of a bruise.

"Oh, my land, child! You poor thing! You know we love having you here. But not at *this* kind of expense. You'd best do as your pa says and stay clear of here."

Kristen nodded. "I know. But I have to talk to you and Mr. Hanchon. I'll only stay a few minutes."

"Well anyway, you came at a good time. John's in the kitchen hungry as a field hand, waiting on his supper. Come along, dear heart, and at least have a cup of cool milk. Seems to me you're losing weight."

The kitchen was spacious and airy and smelled of sourdough mash and strong ash soap. John Hanchon, perched on a sturdy three-legged stool over a deal table, was entering figures in an account ledger by the light of a coal-oil lamp. His long-barreled Henry was propped against the nearest wall.

He closed the ledger when the two women entered. For just a moment the worried frown was not etched quite so deeply into his face.

"Talk about your sight for sore eyes! I swan, there's none prettier than you two anywhere in Paris."

His temporary good mood soured quickly, however, when Kristen explained the purpose of her visit.

"I don't know exactly what Pa's up to," she said. "He was always a private man. But when my mother died, he just ducked inside himself and hasn't come back out once. I don't like to believe that he's breaking the law. But he and Lieutenant Seth Carlson are in on something together, and it involves you. They've been meeting together often lately. They almost always quit talking or change the subject when I'm within hearing.

"I feel awful saying this against my own father,

Mr. Hanchon. But he's taken on plenty of extra hands lately, and I don't see many of them working horses. And after the way Pa carried on about my being here on Sunday, I'm afraid he had something to do with that raid."

"Seth Carlson, huh?" Hanchon nodded, his big, blunt features now lost in thought. "So *that's* what's on the spit. I wondered exactly who Hiram was in cahoots with at the fort. No offense, pretty lady, but I already guessed your pa is mixed up in all this trouble lately. I got no hand-to-God proof, mind you. But he's been on the scrap something fierce ever since I started this spread."

"It's no say-so of his," said Kristen indignantly, "if another man legally trains and sells horses in this territory. Pa can't keep up with the need as it is, and more's wanted every day."

A startled gasp from Sarah interrupted the conversation. "Great day in the morning!"

Kristen glanced in the direction Sarah was staring. For a moment she simply refused to believe what she saw.

Then she screamed.

John Hanchon too glanced toward the door, which had been quietly lifted off its latch. But this wasn't anything like the trouble he'd been expecting, and for a long moment he simply sat there. Then his eyes widened in fear and he lunged for his rifle.

"No, John, you big, handsome fool!" said Sarah. "Don't you know your own son? It's Matthew, or one of them is anyway!"

Corey, his face sheepish at being present at such a time, stepped into the kitchen behind Touch the Sky and Little Horse.

"I figured he had a right to know what's been going on around here," said Corey. "And now Touch—I mean, Matthew, has made up his mind to help you."

"Matthew! It's really you, isn't it, son?"

Sarah moved quickly forward and embraced the youth she had raised as her own, unable to say more. At first, overcome with love for his adopted mother, Touch the Sky forgot his new dignity and restraint as a blooded Cheyenne warrior. He returned his mother's embrace, tears momentarily blurring the room.

Then he remembered himself and glanced quickly toward Little Horse. But this was the smaller Cheyenne's first time inside one of the lodges whites called houses. He was too awed by the novelty of his surroundings to notice his friend's reversion to former ways—or that his parents called him by his paleface name, the name Arrow Keeper had buried in a hole.

"Matthew," said John Hanchon, finally clearing the tight lump from his throat. "It's damn good to see you alive, son."

Only then did Touch the Sky notice, in his bone-numb nervousness, the pretty blonde. He suddenly felt as if the wind had been knocked out of him.

"Kristen?"

"Matthew?"

Their eyes held for a long moment, though he was seeing a familiar memory while she saw a shocking transformation. Like the Hanchons, she couldn't stop gaping at this spectacle: two fierce, young Indians, their bodies muscular and sun-bronzed, the fringes of their leggings spotted with the stiff, black blood of old hunts, old battles.

That was certainly Matthew's face, his distinctive nose and deep-set, perceptive eyes.

But there was also a new confidence and strength about him, places where muscle had hardened, and a distant, wary look in his eyes that Kristen had seen in older men—and wild animals in unfamiliar surroundings. And those scars! Like Sarah, she bit back an exclamation of pity when she noticed the gnarled lines of burn scar on his stomach, the ragged ridge of knife scar high on his chest.

For his part, Touch the Sky felt like he was trying to stand up in a dugout on a raging river. How many times, his heart suffering sharp pangs of loss, had he thought of Kristen? But then, slowly, thoughts of Honey Eater had filled the empty place in his heart. Now, so near again to Kristen, it was as if he had never stopped loving her for even one moment. Was he *not* a Cheyenne then, after all his suffering to earn the name?

"I must go," Kristen said suddenly.

She added, before she could stop herself, "And you, Matthew. It's not safe for you around here! You shouldn't've come back. Please leave before my pa hears about it!"

She muttered a hasty good-bye and was gone before Touch the Sky could reply. Corey left too, saying his pa must be on the warpath by now.

As they had agreed, Touch the Sky introduced Little Horse as War Eagle, avoiding his real name. Little Horse kept his eyes cast down at the floor when spoken to by John or Sarah—not out of disrespect, but because he believed an Indian's soul could be stolen if he made eye contact with whites.

For nearly two hours, the Hanchons kept their

son busy with eager questions. But despite their obvious joy at seeing him again, they were clearly troubled by Kristen's parting warning.

"Kristen was right, son," said Sarah after she had fed everyone fried potatoes and side meat and cornbread. "I'm so happy to see you I could just burst! But it isn't safe for you around here. Seems like trouble's been happening ten ways a second lately. You and your friend risked enough just by riding here."

"Your mother's giving it to you straight," said Hanchon. "There's no real law out here and scarcely any gum'ment except the Army. And I reckon you already know how much the Army will help us. Hiram Steele is mean and low and spiteful, the brooding kind that holds a grudge until it hollers mama. And he grudges me every honest dollar I earn. You should clear out tonight, under cover of darkness."

Dutifully, Touch the Sky translated these warnings to Little Horse. His friend was still devouring hot slabs of cornbread as quick as Sarah pulled them from the oven. He listened with an impassive face as Touch the Sky explained the danger in remaining there.

Then Little Horse shrugged.

"Brother, when have we *not* faced danger? We are Indians and we live like the buffalo, always hunted, killed for sport. Only, tell me this one thing. This paleface girl with hair like morning sunshine, I saw how you two looked at each other. Have you held her in your blanket and made love talk?"

Touch the Sky's troubled face answered the question clearly enough.

"Brother," said Little Horse sternly, "we are

warriors and we have come to grease our enemy's bones with war paint! *That* is our mission and we must hold our purpose close to our hearts. This golden-haired squaw, I sense danger if you let her into your thoughts. You are a Cheyenne, and Honey Eater waits for you back at Yellow Bear's camp!"

"What did War Eagle say?" asked Sarah when Little Horse quit speaking.

Touch the Sky felt thoroughly miserable. But at least Little Horse's impassive face and tone made the lie easy.

"He said that he's never tasted anything so good as your cornbread!"

All through the day Honey Eater had listened to the hypnotic rhythm of chanting, to the rustling rattle of snake teeth in dried gourds.

He was slipping away, ravaged by the red-speckled cough, but Chief Yellow Bear was still alive. Honey Eater had fresh cause for worry: The only nourishment her father could hold down now was hot yarrow tea with wild bee honey. But he was still alive, and for this Honey Eater gave thanks to the sun and sky and the four directions of the wind.

She stepped past the flap of the tipi she shared with her father. The evening air felt cool and fresh after the thick smoke of the interior, where dog-wood incense was kept burning day and night. The days were gradually growing warmer and longer. Soon they would enter The Moon When the Ponies Shed.

Today, as usual, she picked fresh columbine and pressed it between wet leaves. Then she returned to the tipi and placed it near her robes. In the morning she would braid her hair with it.

Despite the sad vigil for Yellow Bear, daily life in camp went on as always. The young men wrestled and ran foot and pony races, sometimes all night until dawn; the children threw stones at birds and staged mock battles; the women talked and cooked. In the still, quiet hours of darkness, the old grandmothers and new widows mourned their dead with sad songs and chants.

Things went on as usual, even though Touch the Sky had coolly ridden out of her life! Now she could still hear the harsh calls of willets and grebes and hawks, the softer warblings of orioles and thrushes and purple finches. But since he had left her alone in this terrible time, none of it was anything but noise.

Arrow Keeper had told her little about why Touch the Sky left. Whatever trouble called him away, could his former life be more important than his life now as a Cheyenne? Did he not realize how vulnerable she would be if Yellow Bear crossed over to the Land of Ghosts? Surely he knew the decree of tribal law, that no young woman could live on her own but only with a father, a brother, or a husband. She had no brother, and soon she would have no father. If Black Elk again sent her the gift of horses, how could she refuse?

These thoughts skittered around inside her head like frenzied rodents. Now, as she stoked the embers to life under the cooking tripod, she noticed several of the clan Headmen walking toward the council lodge. Other males, all warriors or elders, also drifted across camp toward the lodge. She knew they must be meeting in formal council—they wore their best ornamental clothing, decorated with porcupine quills, stones, feathers, hair from enemy scalps.

"Honey Eater."

The sudden words startled her. She turned around to confront a fierce-eyed young warrior dressed in battle finery, complete with feathered war bonnet.

"I would speak with you before the council begins."

"I always have ears for your words, Black Elk."

"But *do* you? When I speak, do you truly place my words next to your heart? Or are they like pesky gnats, which bother you a moment until you slap them away from your ears and then forget them?"

Black Elk's bonnet was full of the eagle feathers of bravery. There was a dead flap of leathery skin where one ear had been torn off in battle, then later sewn back onto his skull with buckskin thread.

"What does Black Elk mean by this odd question?"

"You play the fox well, little one! You know I speak of Touch the Sky. The entire tribe knows that you have declared your love for this stranger who rides among us reeking of the white man's stink! But you must turn stone ears to his love talk. Even now, despite Arrow Keeper's objections, the Headmen are meeting to discuss his and Little Horse's desertion."

"He has not deserted his tribe!" said Honey Eater. "He is a brave and strong warrior."

"Would you tell this thing to me, who trained him? I will not speak in a wolf bark against him. He *is* brave and strong. With a handful of bucks like him, what battles I could win! He spoke brave love talk to you when the paleface dogs held you prisoner and tortured him in their camp. And yes, he has respectfully cut short his hair to mourn our dead. But a dog that walks on two legs is still a dog, not a Cheyenne.

"Bravery and strength are good things, but they are not enough. Looking like a Cheyenne is not enough. There is also loyalty to the tribe, duty, discipline. He was not raised a Cheyenne. In his heart he is white. This is why he so easily deserts us now to join them. In his heart he is still our enemy!"

The next moment Black Elk turned his back on her protests and headed toward the council lodge.

The lodge fell silent for a moment when Black Elk lifted the flap aside and stepped inside. This silence was a mark of respect for the young brave Yellow Bear had named as their battle chief.

Arrow Keeper sat in the center of the lodge, wrapped in his blanket. The voting Headmen filled nearly one half of the lodge. The younger warriors, who could speak but were not yet permitted to vote with the stones, occupied the other half.

Arrow Keeper, their acting peace chief, lit the common clay pipe and passed it on. After all who wished to had smoked, Arrow Keeper began the council.

"Brothers! The cold moons were harsh. Now what game can be found is lean and snow-starved. The meat is stringy, with no juice or tasty fat.

"Cheyennes, today these old hands carry no weapons. But I fought Utes beside Yellow Bear and buried my wife and children after the Pawnee raid at Wolf Creek. I have smoked the common pipe with you, and duty instructs me to speak only things that matter. So I say only this, that when game is short, tempers grow short. When there is hunger in the belly for meat, there is hunger in the spirit for blood! Do not punish Touch the Sky and Little Horse simply because of your hunger and bloodlust."

"But Father!" said Wolf Who Hunts Smiling. "You are brave and wise, but you speak in riddles. Think what they have done. Our chief is about to enter the Land of Ghosts. Even a hen will remain at the nest to fight for her chicks! Yet will these two 'warriors' fight for Cheyenne children?"

Wolf Who Hunts Smiling was a warrior now, one of the youngest in the tribe. He wore scalps dangling from his clout and practiced the fierce dignity and restraint he had learned from his older cousin, Black Elk.

Arrow Keeper folded his arms until the lodge had quieted. Now Black Elk rose.

"Fathers! Brothers! I do not question the manly courage of Little Horse or Touch the Sky. However, both are weak in judgment. And perhaps we were too hasty in presenting the blue feather to Firetop. Has he not abused our token of friendship? Has he not used his special place among us to entice away two of our best warriors to fight white men's battles. True it is, he showed bravery in helping us fight the lice-eaters. But is it not also true that the Indian can *never* trust the paleface?"

"Our war chief speaks the straight word," said Swift Canoe, who, as always, sat beside Wolf Who Hunts Smiling. "I have heard much about Touch the Sky's bravery after he was captured in the paleface camp. But did he not willfully disobey Black Elk's orders, which led to his capture *and* the death of our brother, High Forehead?"

"These words ring clear," said Wolf Who Hunts Smiling. "And who has actually seen most of the brave deeds Touch the Sky claims to have performed? Just because he fought the white sellers of strong water, this is no proof he is not a spy for the Bluecoats. The palefaces too war among themselves just as the red men do. I still believe he is a spy!"

Again old Arrow Keeper was forced to fold his arms to quiet the excited buzzing in the lodge. He longed to answer the young Cheyenne's unjust accusations. Arrow Keeper and Honey Eater were the only witnesses when Touch the Sky killed the Pawnee leader War Thunder, saving Yellow Bear's life. But they were both forced to remain silent—the rest of the tribe knew they favored the new arrival. Any support from them would only harden the others against him even more.

The medicine man sensed what was coming next. The younger warriors would demand a vote to permanently ostracize Touch the Sky, and perhaps even Little Horse, from the tribe. But a stroke of recent good fortune had suggested an alternative plan to Arrow Keeper: For the duration of the next moon, Chief Sun Dance of the Lakota Sioux had moved his clan circles just across the river from their Cheyenne cousins. This was only a temporary move while they hunted elk in the foothills of the Bighorns. But the presence of so many fierce Sioux warriors made attack from any Cheyenne enemies unlikely.

This meant that some braves could now be spared. Now, before Touch the Sky's enemies could move to expel him forever, Arrow Keeper spoke up.

"Brothers! The wildcat fights, or it flees. It is time to either expose Touch the Sky for a spy or lay these charges behind him forever. I suggest a plan.

"Our number is now swollen by Lakotas. Therefore, let us send two capable young bucks to report on Touch the Sky's activities. If he is a spy, surely we can find this thing out now. If so, his enemies may kill him as tribal law decrees! If not, his enemies must cease forever to speak in a wolf bark toward him."

Arrow Keeper's plan was practical, yet just, and met with strong voice approval. Both Swift Canoe and Wolf Who Hunts Smiling volunteered to go. But Arrow Keeper stubbornly shook his head. He reminded the others that Wolf Who Hunts Smiling had walked between Touch the Sky and the fire. And Swift Canoe still blamed the death of his brother on Touch the Sky.

To avoid rebellion from the young warriors, Arrow Keeper knew at least one of Touch the Sky's enemies would have to go. But he insisted that the other must be someone neutral toward Touch the Sky. Finally it was decided that River of Winds, whose medicine bundle was the rattlesnake, would accompany Swift Canoe.

Now, thought Arrow Keeper, *I have done my best.* The rest was up to Maiyun, the Supernatural. Arrow Keeper still believed in the powerful vision at sacred Medicine Lake, which foretold a warrior's glory for Touch the Sky.

But it was a terrible place Touch the Sky was now trapped in, caught between the sap and the bark. Had he cut all ties to the white man only to be savagely murdered by the red man?

Chapter Six

Two sleeps after the Cheyenne council voted to send spies to the south, John Hanchon showed Touch the Sky and Little Horse the lay of his mustang spread.

Before they left, Wade McKenna had been called up to the house. The tough old Irish foreman had lived in the territory for ten years. He recognized the tall, broad-shouldered redskin buck as the quiet kid who used to work for his adopted white parents at Hanchon's mercantile. McKenna never even batted an eye when he was asked to pass the word to all the hands: If you come across Cheyenne Indians on or near Hanchon land, don't pull down on them. They're flying our colors.

It was well after sunset, but a full moon painted the grass silver and made riding easy. The three stayed abreast except when forced to ride single file through narrow defiles. They were close enough to the river to hear the steady chuckle of the current, made more lively by spring runoff. Before them, the lush bottomland rose gradually into gentle hills dotted with stands of juniper and scrub pine.

John Hanchon reined in his roan cutting horse. He sat his saddle, gazing out toward the vast summer pasture.

"So help me Hannah, son, it's just now sinking in. First the store, now this place. A man doesn't bust his hump just for the love of sweat. I was hoping to put by against the future, mainly for your ma's sake after I'm gone. Now I see how close I am to losing everything. I've worked until I'm mule-tired, but I still go to bed scared every night. Scared your ma will be taking in washing after I'm planted."

Hanchon shook off his pensive mood and became all business.

"This is where the summer pasture starts," he said, pointing with a vast sweep of his arm. "Most of the mustangs are grazing out of sight behind the line shack on top that shoulder. See it? You could maybe sleep there except that Woody Monroe, the line rider, isn't too partial to Indians. You sure you won't stay up at the house with us?"

Touch the Sky shook his head. The rest of the hands were not all as likely as Wade to accept the presence of Indians so close to the bunkhouse. And no point in mentioning that Little Horse would never sleep in any paleface lodge.

"If word gets out," he said, "that Cheyennes are anywhere near the house, they'll be sure to burn it to the ground this time. From up here we can watch the horses and the approaches to the house."

There was no denying this. Hanchon nodded. "Well, since that last raid I got a guard set up for the yard and main corrals. We'll be safe enough. But if you two got your minds set on mixing into this, you'll need rifles. Ride back to the house with me and I'll loan you a couple."

Later, Touch the Sky thought, perhaps he would tell his father what happened to the rifle he took when he first left Bighorn Falls a year ago—how it had been given to Wolf Who Hunts Smiling when the intruder named Matthew Hanchon was declared a spy.

"I wonder," said Hanchon, mostly to himself as he glanced toward the dark line shack again, "why Woody hasn't lit his lamp and stove yet? Prob'ly still grouping the herd for the night. Sometimes they'll scatter to hell 'n' gone up into the high country."

They held their horses to a long trot and quickly returned to the house. Hanchon waited until Sarah left to tend to the wounded man staying in the lean-to bedroom built off the rear of the house. Then he unlocked a sturdy oak gun cabinet in the front parlor.

"I kept these when the mercantile went bust," he said. "Take your pick. Wade will set you up with powder and ball and percussion caps. You can fire them tomorrow when it's light, get your wind and elevation."

Touch the Sky hefted a percussion-action Sharps, then a .44-caliber North and Savage revolving-cylinder rifle.

"The trigger guard is combined with the lever," explained Hanchon. "When you move it, you revolve the cylinder and cock the hammer."

Touch the Sky liked the balance of the Sharps better. Little Horse owned a scattergun, acquired when he defended himself against the miner Enis McGillycuddy. But the tribe had no skins to trade for shells and ammunition, and he had left it behind. Now he chose a four-barrel flintlock shotgun. The barrels, each equipped with its own pan and frizzen, were rotated by hand. Little Horse smiled at the sharp, precise clicks as each barrel snapped into place.

"Tell your friend," said Hanchon to his son, "that a man could toss a biscuit farther than that piece shoots. But close up, one shot will strip the clothes off three men standing shoulder to shoulder."

As the two Cheyennes rode back out through the moonlit yard, the hired hand riding sentry by the horse-breaking pen stared at them as if they were a rare circus act. The warriors proudly ignored him.

"You boys want to buy a saddle?" the hand called out behind them. "Sell it to you heap cheap. Then you can ride in style without gettin' blisters on your sitter."

"Brother," said Little Horse after Touch the Sky had translated the hand's remark, "look at this thing."

They halted at one corner of the horse-breaking pen and Little Horse pointed inside. Touch the Sky spotted a small white mustang. Its muscular flanks were bloody from being viciously roweled, its eyes wild from a day of being choked to break it to the harness.

"Why," said Little Horse, "must the white man break a horse's spirit when he trains it? The red man cannot understand this. Because we do not break their spirit, our ponies are superior in battle. I have seen our elders lead a vicious horse miles away to deep sand, where it cannot buck its rider, rather than beat the animal into submission."

"It is as Arrow Keeper told me," said Touch the Sky. "I saw it myself growing up among them. It is not the paleface way to respect nature. They must always defeat her and her creatures, just as they must always defeat each other. See how this man Steele works to destroy my father?"

As the two Cheyennes pointed their mounts toward the summer graze, Touch the Sky again felt John Hanchon's words gnawing at him like a chancre: *I've worked until I'm mule-tired, but I still go to bed scared every night.*

They made camp just beneath a thickly forested ridge overlooking the summer pasture and the outlying line shack. They chose a thick stand of wind-twisted juniper which formed a windbreak near a cold seep spring. This site would permit a small fire and provide a natural bulwark against attack if they were surprised.

Then, while Little Horse slipped off into the forest to set a few snares for rabbits, Touch the Sky gathered wood. He removed a piece of flint from his legging sash and struck fire from it with his knife. He made the campfire Indian style by burning the logs from the ends, not the middle, to avoid wasting wood.

The location of the Grandmother Star to the north told them night was well advanced by the time they had tethered their ponies and let the fire burn down for the night. By the flickering light of the dying flames, Little Horse sharpened his knife against a flat stone. Touch the Sky used a bone awl and split-sinew thread to mend his extra moccasins. The sinew was a little tough at first, but he softened it in his mouth with saliva.

Twice he pricked his fingers deep, distracted by constant thoughts of Kristen—thoughts he had once believed were smoke behind him. But after seeing her again today, he couldn't help contrasting her golden, nimbus-haired looks to Honey Eater's dusky beauty.

Nor could he help wondering to which race he owed his heart and his life. Old Knobby, the hostler in Bighorn Falls, had insisted the red man and white man could never live together in peace. But why? Why must he choose one group and turn his back on the other?

Suddenly a horse whickered, cutting into his thoughts. The sound did not come from the herd behind them but from the line shack below.

"Brother!" said Little Horse in a tense whisper. "A rider approaches our camp!"

Quick as a blink they were both out of their robes and had backed into the surrounding brush, abandoning the circle of remaining light around the fire. Touch the Sky eased back the hammer of the Sharps and felt to make sure a primer cap was centered in the loading gate.

A moment later a saddled but riderless horse walked into the camp clearing. The girth had been uncinched under its belly, and the saddle had slipped halfway toward the ground, one stirrup dragging.

The horse, clearly hungry for human company, nuzzled Touch the Sky's shoulder when he stepped out from hiding.

"The owner was jumped while saddling or unsaddling," said Little Horse. "But who is it?"

At the same moment, both Cheyennes glanced downridge toward the dark line shack. Still no sign of fire or light.

"I think," said Touch the Sky, "it is time to check on this paleface who does not like Indians."

He quickly unsaddled the horse and pointed it toward the main corrals below, slapping it hard on the flank to send it running. He knew that, unsaddled, it would return on its own to the barn it was used to. Its arrival should alert the hands to send help.

Their uncle the moon still shone brightly, making secret progress difficult across the open expanse. As Black Elk had taught them, they rubbed their bodies with saliva, then smeared their wet skin with sand to cut reflection. Rifles would slow them down, so they chose their knives instead. Then, relying on isolated trees and bushes, they made their way on foot to the shack.

The door, caught in a steady breeze, repeatedly banged open and shut as they sneaked up from the rear. Touch the Sky eased around one corner, Little Horse the other. They saw him at the same time—a man lying spread-eagle in front of the shack, jaw slacked open as if he were drunk.

But the paleface wasn't drunk. His right temple was a raw, pulpy mess, as if he'd been struck hard with a rifle butt.

Touch the Sky gently shook him. The line rider groaned but remained unconscious.

"The blood is dark and crusting," said Little Horse. "He was attacked earlier. Much earlier."

Touch the Sky nodded. He squatted to examine the matted grass in front of the shack. It had been well trampled within the past few hours by many well-shod horses, as many as six or seven. But where were the riders now, and why had they come?

Perhaps thinking the same thing, Little Horse lowered his voice even more and said, "Brother, think on this thing. These men may have come even as your white father first showed us this lodge and wondered why it was so dark. They may have ridden on up to gather horses, only waiting for the moon to hide his bright face a bit so they may drive them out of the valley."

"Which means," said Touch the Sky, "they may have seen us make camp. They may know we are here."

Both youths were disheartened at this prospect. Only dead Cheyennes, Black Elk had insisted over and over, lost the advantage of surprise.

"It also means," said Little Horse, "that they may be very near, right now. Watching us."

"The wind is from the sun's resting place," said Touch the Sky.

Little Horse nodded, understanding. They stepped away from the shack, faced into the wind blowing from the pasture to the west. For several minutes they stood stone silent, stone still, simply smelling the wind.

At first Touch the Sky smelled only the sweet grass, the clean, woman smell of mountain laurel, faint cooking odors lingering in the shack. Then, gradually, he became aware of something else: the musty stink of leather-shod horses and white men.

Little Horse met his eyes and nodded. He smelled it too.

No words were exchanged. It was nighttime,

and they both understood that no Cheyenne who expected to live ever attacked a foe at night. Now they needed to observe while this fat moon aided them.

They stuck close to bushes and trees and ducked behind hummocks, crossing open expanses on their elbows and knees. They leapfrogged, one dashing ahead to cover and then waiting for the other to join him before moving on. Steadily they worked their way along the ridge and around the shoulder of the hill.

Little Horse was about to scramble into a coulee when he suddenly froze in his tracks and lifted his hand to halt Touch the Sky.

Touch the Sky edged up beside him. Little Horse pointed further into the dry gulch. A half-dozen men waited there, their horses picketed nearby. One man squatted on his rowels, smoking. Several others shared a bottle of whiskey. They looked bored and impatient.

Below them, on the other side of the wide coulee, hundreds of mustangs were bunched together in the moonlight. Steep-sloping hills formed a natural pen on three sides. The only way out was through the coulee.

"By hell, I'm tired of waiting," said the man smoking the cigarette. He flipped his butt away in a wide arc and rose to his feet, spurs jingling. "I say let's point 'em out of here now, moon or no. We got 'em bunched good now, but they won't stay that way forever."

"Winslow, you work us too damn hard," said one of the men passing the whiskey bottle around. "You hadn't spooked that wrangler's horse, we wouldn't be in such a damned all-fire hurry, would we?"

"Last I checked, that hoss was just wandering the ridge," said another man. "With the saddle on, it'll stick close."

"Maybe so. But I ain't heisting skittish mustangs in full moonlight."

"Anyhow," said Winslow, pointing north, "there's clouds boiling up over yonder, heading straight for the moon. Just a little longer and we can push 'em out of here."

The man called Winslow was tall and string-bean thin with shaggy hair the color of wet sand. Something about his voice alerted Touch the Sky. He strained his eyes in the clear moonlight, watching as Winslow turned in profile.

The man's face was badly pockmarked from smallpox. A moment later Touch the Sky remembered him, and a cold, numbing hatred iced his limbs. He glanced at several others and recognized two of them.

Touch the Sky and Little Horse had fought these hardcases before, further north in Plains Indian country. They were former members of the private "army" paid by the whiskey trader Henri Lagace! But the army had disbanded after the Cheyenne raid on their camp which led to Touch the Sky's killing Lagace.

Clearly, Hiram Steele had found good use for unemployed cutthroats.

Little Horse jabbed his shoulder excitedly, and Touch the Sky realized that his friend too had recognized their former enemies.

They backed slowly away from the rim of the coulee and held quick council behind a huge boulder.

"Brother," said Little Horse, glancing over his shoulder into the sky, "soon the moon goes into hiding. Under cover of darkness, the white dogs will easily drive the ponies. Without our ponies, we cannot run for help in time."

"These are the white-livered cowards who killed High Forehead and the rest of our brothers," said Touch the Sky. "They invaded our camp and killed children and elders. Now they land like carrion birds to destroy my white parents! We cannot let them succeed."

"I have ears for your words and courage to back them. But we cannot anger Maiyun by raising our battle axes after dark! We must play the fox, not the lion."

Touch the Sky nodded. Both youths knew full well what had to be done and the best way of doing it. They circled wide around the mustang-filled clearing, hugging the steep slopes. At some places they were forced to cling to scrub pine to avoid sliding down the slope. But they made good time, unobserved, and were soon behind the mustang herd.

Little Horse nudged him as they crouched low, trying not to spook the herd too soon with their human scent now that the wind was behind them.

"I am quicker on my feet than you," he said. "And you make the noise better. Let me get closer. I will scatter them while you make the call."

A heartbeat later Little Horse was gone, already blending into the herd and slapping flanks left and right.

All horses everywhere, Black Elk had assured his warriors many times, are frightened senseless by bears. Now Touch the Sky swallowed a huge breath and brought it back out from deep in his guts, making a noise that was half bark, half growl—the deep, menacing woof of the grizzly.

Instantly, scores of horses reared in panic, then bolted for the coulee. The ground thundered and vibrated, divots of soil flew everywhere.

Touch the Sky again loosed his guttural imitation of a prowling grizzly. Now and again he caught a momentary glimpse of Little Horse, still smacking mustangs. Only the small Cheyenne's quick, sure movements saved him from being trampled as he leaped first left, then right, twirling just out of harm's way.

Above the thundering din, Touch the Sky heard the white men shouting and cursing. They wisely decided to flee rather than attempt to halt the panicked herd as it squeezed itself into the gulch, threatening to crush them.

He found Little Horse covered with dirt but unharmed. The two grinned in triumph. They knew the herd would scatter once it cleared the coulee on the other side, drifting back eventually to the lusher pastures of the high country. A light burned at the line shack, where someone was tending to the injured Woody Monroe. And shouts from further down the valley announced that wranglers at the Hanchon spread had been alerted to the rustlers. Winslow and his friends would count themselves lucky if they cleared the valley alive.

But as they returned to their camp, the two Cheyennes sobered quickly. The shock of once again meeting their hated enemies filled them with grim determination to triumph.

"Brother," said Little Horse later, before Touch the Sky drifted down a long tunnel into sleep, "I recall well how those paleface devils piled hot rocks on you and laughed as you were about to swallow the Sioux arrow. I recall well the suffering they caused our tribe. This is no longer a white man's battle I am helping you fight. And I swear this: Either we defeat them, or we will die the glorious death trying!"

Chapter Seven

"Damn it all, man!" said Hiram Steele, snapping his watch shut and returning it to the fob pocket of his vest. "Couldn't you get here sooner with the news? It's too late to warn Winslow and the rest."

"Get here sooner? I'm damn lucky to even be alive," said Seth Carlson. "Before I could leave the post, I had to file a report on the skirmish. And there was clerical work to do on the wounded trooper. He broke an arm when one of the bucks knocked him off his horse. Not to mention that I had to get medical care myself and requisition a new horse."

Steele barely wasted a glance on the patch, the size of a silver dollar, where skin had been scraped off Carlson's face in the prairie-dog-hole mishap. The rancher paced before the fieldstone fireplace, his heavy boots thudding on the bare planks. The flint-gray eyes focused on nothing, lost in worry.

"You're sure it was him?" said Steele. "All Injuns look alike."

"It was the Hanchon boy, all right. I didn't recognize the buck with him."

"So it was just the two?"

Carlson nodded. "And Corey Robinson, though he wasn't fool enough to fight against us. All he did was rabbit."

"Hell, two pissant redskins and a freckle-faced sprout don't put snow in *my* boots."

"Maybe, but I don't like the turn this trail is taking," said Carlson. "This is more than I bargained on. Today that red bastard humiliated me in front of my men. And because of him I had to shoot the best horse I've owned since I drew orders to this hellhole!"

"I'll give you a better horse. After this raid tonight, you can have your pick. As for that buck humiliating you, don't forget the shoot-to-kill order. He'll get his comeuppance soon enough."

If all went as planned, thought Steele, a good portion of Hanchon's best horseflesh would soon be scattered among the herds grazing Steele property. No brands were used until the horses were broken and ready to sell, so Hanchon would have no legal claim against him.

"Just a warning," said Carlson. "Harding checked up in his orders manual, said something about having to maybe appoint a military board of inquiry to look into this Indian problem. If Hanchon reports this raid, there might be someone from the fort nosing around, asking you and your men questions."

Steele shrugged his beefy shoulders. "Anybody asks any of my wranglers, they were all in the bunkhouse tonight playing dominoes and checkers."

"That's just fine for you and your men," said the young lieutenant, irritation clear in his voice. "But who covers *my* back-trail? I've been submitting false reconnaissance reports. If Harding ever gets wind of it, I'm headed for the stockade. Harding is no Indian-lover, and brains are not his strong suit. But he lives by the book."

Steele had a hair-trigger temper and did not usually tolerate ill temper from others. For a moment, the resentment in Seth Carlson's tone made angry blood throb in his temples. But then he reconsidered. He needed Carlson's influence at the fort.

"Look here," he said reasonably, "no need to get on the peck. Harding doesn't know sic-'em about what we're up to."

"I'll grant that. Harding wouldn't notice his own reflection in a hall of mirrors."

"All right, then. We'll just keep Major Harding flummoxed like we been doing all along. You been blaming all this ruckus lately on renegade Cheyennes, right? And didn't two just ride into the territory today raising hell and wounding soldiers?"

Carlson had already told himself all this. What really pricked at him like a burr in his boot was the fact that the Hanchon boy was back—and that Kristen had evidently known he was coming and gone to meet him.

"Do you remember," he said, "when we talked about posting a sentry on Thompson's Bluff overlooking the Hanchon spread?"

Steele nodded.

"I checked with him before I rode out here. The two Injun bucks and Corey Robinson rode to the Hanchon place, all right. But just before they arrived, Kristen showed up there too."

For a moment Steele simply stared in disbelief, as if Carlson had just announced that pigs could fly. Then, all of an instant, his broad, bluff face flushed purple with rage. But his voice was deadly calm when he finally spoke.

"You're not seriously telling me that my daughter went out to the Hanchon spread *today*?"

"Unless there's another pretty blonde hereabouts who rides a swayback piebald."

"Did she meet with the Indian?"

"The sentry can't see their place from the bluff, not the yard. Just the wagon road leading out to it. But she had to see him. She was still there when he rode in."

Steele was struck dumb with disbelief. He stopped pacing for a moment as he fought down the urge to rush back to Kristen's bedroom and drag her out by the hair. Hadn't he already warned the girl—twice, by God!—to steer clear of that place?

Obviously, trying to keep a woman on the straight and narrow was like trying to train a cat. Threats were useless with Kristen, she was too bullheaded. But nobody bucked Hiram Steele, not even his own daughter.

He glanced at Carlson. The officer's injured face was still twisted in a petulant frown. Maybe it was time to throw the dog a bone, and at the same time punish Kristen.

"They say," said Steele, thinking out loud, "that if you're on the plains and you have no tree for hanging a man, you can always drag-hang him."

Carlson's frown turned from anger to puzzlement. "Could you spell that out clearer?"

"Just wait here," said Steele, heading back toward Kristen's bedroom. "You'll soon catch my drift."

Kristen lifted the chimney from the coal-oil lamp and lit the wick with a sulphur match.

Light splashed the rose-patterned carpet and pushed shadows back into the corners of her room. She opened the top drawer of a sturdy pine dresser and tugged aside a neatly folded calico skirt. Then she removed a packet of letters tied with a bit of red silk ribbon—letters from Matthew Hanchon. Letters he used to leave, in their secret meeting place, on those awful days when he delivered supplies and she couldn't manage to meet him.

She knew Seth Carlson had just arrived. That's why she had feigned sleepiness and slipped back to her room earlier than usual. Now, as she again read some of the letters, she could faintly hear her father and Carlson's voices, like sounds carried on the wind.

Her thoughts and feelings had been a confused riot ever since unexpectedly seeing Matthew earlier today. Before, when he'd lived his former life in Bighorn Falls, she had always known, of course, that Matthew was different. But seeing him this way—today—made that difference so stark and real.

The way he was dressed, those awful scars, that new glint of hard mettle in his eyes—and the strange language he spoke with that other Cheyenne! All of it made her realize how impossible was this love she still felt. He couldn't live in her world, nor she in his, any more than a hawk could nest with a falcon.

And yet, despite his fearsome, savage aspect today, she couldn't help thinking about how magnificent he had looked. Stronger, more confident, with that heightened sense of alertness which characterized frontier survivors.

While her fancy coined these ideas, three quick taps on her door startled her.

"Kristen?"

Her heart leaped into her throat. Her father never visited her room unless it was something serious.

"Yes, Pa?"

"You dressed?"

"No," she lied.

"Well, put some clothes on. Then come out front. I got something to say to you."

Kristen's brow furrowed in a frown of confusion. Her father's voice was low, composed, calm—frighteningly so.

She put the letters away and waited a few minutes until her breathing was under control. But her pulse quickened again when she found that Carlson too was waiting in the front parlor, seated in a ladderback chair. He rose smartly when she entered, trying to keep the injured side of his face out of her sight.

"Miss Hanchon. I hope you're well?"

"As well as a body can be when she's tugged out of bed."

Despite her bravado, Kristen was so scared her limbs trembled. Her father was being oddly polite and formal with her. Some disaster loomed, and she knew by now that it had something to do with her forbidden visit to the Hanchons. But despite being prepared, she felt his next words with the force of hard slaps.

"Did you have a good time with your friend Matthew Hanchon today?"

"I—I don't—"

Warm blood rushed into her face and she blushed deep to the roots of her hair. What her father was suggesting was a lie, but the shock of the confrontation made her feel guilty.

Steele read his daughter's blush as a confession. Rage sparked in his eyes for a moment. Then they went dull and flat and calculating.

Carlson too read her blush as a confession. Indignant anger welled up inside him. Wasn't she always high-hatting him and looking down her nose like she was quality goods? Yet here she was, admitting to consorting with a savage redskin!

"It crosses my mind more and more lately," said Hiram, "how easy a young girl can go astray out here in the wilderness. Especially a young girl without a mother or older sisters to guide her."

When her father actually smiled, Kristen knew she faced a crisis.

"Lieutenant Carlson has requested the honor of your hand in marriage. I've given my blessing to the union."

Carlson started and moved to the edge of his chair, then settled back again and assumed a poker face. Steele winked at him, then turned to his daughter again.

"Wha'd'you say to that, girl? Think you'll be a good Army wife?"

Kristen's mouth felt dry and stuffed with cotton. She swallowed hard.

"I've never given it any thought."

She was staring at Carlson as she said this. Some of his former servility returned to his tone as he said, "Your pa's not trying to sell you a bill of goods tonight, of course. You'll want time to think on it."

Her icy tone strained her father's smile, but he only widened it before he said, "Well, you best *start* thinking about it. The day's coming quick when you're gonna have to choose. Life as an officer's wife on the frontier, or moving back to Providence to stay with my sister Thelma."

A shudder moved up Kristen's spine like a cold finger. She recalled her spinster Aunt Thelma's talcumed face and stale-as-dust old-lady smell.

"It'll have to be one or the other," said Steele. "A white girl that hobnobs with murdering redskins is wanting looking after."

"Murdering! Matthew Hanchon is no murderer!"

"Who do you think killed Boone Wilson, the Queen of England?"

"If he did, it was self-defense, not murder."

"When a daughter of mine," said Steele, "takes up with Indians against her own people, that's the day I wish I'd died as a child. You're going to make up your mind and make it up quick. Either you marry Seth Carlson or you move to your Aunt Thelma's. And you better write this on your pillowcase. If I hear of you visiting the Hanchon spread or meeting with that redskin bastard of theirs again, you'll *have* to get married because you sure's hell won't have a home here!"

Chapter Eight

His eyelids eased open from deep sleep. At first, before the last cobwebs of slumber were swept from his eyes, Touch the Sky didn't recognize where he was.

He saw a wall of wind-bent juniper trees slightly below him on the sloping ground, felt the dew in the grass where his arms lay outside of his buffalo robe. The weak light and warmth of the sun told him it was still early. Then he suddenly remembered everything and rolled over to wake Little Horse. But his friend's robe was empty.

And less than a pace from Touch the Sky stood a Bluecoat officer!

He recalled the warning the corporal had given him yesterday: *We got orders to shoot all Cheyennes on sight!*

Instinctively one of Touch the Sky's hands patted the doeskin pouch on his breechclout. It held the badger claws Arrow Keeper told him were the magic totem of his clan.

His medicine bundle was safe. The very same moment, remembering not to signal his intention in his eyes, he kicked his robe aside and rolled hard into the Bluecoat intruder's legs.

The officer fell heavily, cursing, then rolled free with amazing quickness and strength. Touch the Sky leaped after him and wrestled him down again. They grappled, rolling through the wet grass, crashing through small bushes.

The Cheyenne finally slipped a powerful choke-hold on his adversary. The next moment he felt an explosion of fiery pain as the pony soldier brought a short but accurate knee thrust up into his groin. This loosened his choke, but he refused to let the soldier squirm out from under him.

For a moment they were locked eyeball to eyeball, both gasping for breath as they struggled for dominance. The Cheyenne's face was an impassive mask except for the determined slit of his mouth. The Bluecoat's face, in contrast, twisted into a fierce scowl.

The soldier slumped under him for a moment, and Touch the Sky managed to slip the obsidian knife from its sheath. Despite the shoot-to-kill order, however, he couldn't bring himself to plunge the blade home. The Bluecoat wore a sidearm but had not once tried to draw it. A Cheyenne was honor-bound to keep the sacred Medicine Arrows forever sweet and clean by killing only those who tried to kill him.

When Touch the Sky suddenly raised the knife, the Bluecoat's eyes mirrored fear.

The Cheyenne hurled the knife, point first, into the ground just beside the officer's head.

"Christ on a mule! Get off him, Matthew, you tarnal fool! That's Tom Riley!"

In his excitement, Corey forgot to use his friend's Cheyenne name. Now he burst out from the trees above them, still tucking in his shirttail after relieving himself.

At the same moment, Little Horse stepped out past the tree line carrying a pair of dead rabbits. He saw the Bluecoat and Touch the Sky, still apparently engaged in combat, before he spotted Corey. He dropped the game and raced toward them, unsheathing his knife.

"No, brother!" said Touch the Sky in Cheyenne. "He is Firetop's friend!"

Little Horse managed to avert his knife. But he had too much momentum going to avoid colliding with the two on the ground. Moments later all three rose from the tangled confusion of arms and legs.

Corey swooped double in sudden laughter.

"Ain't you three a fine pack of scrappers! You look like a bug with too many legs!"

"I told you to wake him up first," said Riley. He picked up his bent-brim hat and slapped the dust off it. His sunburned face turned even redder as he flushed with sheepishness. "I tried to tell you," he said to Touch the Sky, "but you wouldn't let me catch my wind."

"Touch the Sky, this is Tom Riley. Though I reckon you two've already met. Tom, this here is Touch the Sky's friend Little Horse. He don't speak English."

Riley knew enough about Plains Indians customs not to be offended when neither man looked him square in the eye. He caught himself before he offered his hand.

"Your pa told us where you planned to camp," Corey said to Touch the Sky. "Tom's got some news. Bad news."

While Little Horse dressed out the rabbits and roasted them on a green stick, Riley explained what he had overheard at the fort when Corey was riding north to Yellow Bear's camp. It was no surprise, of course, that Hiram Steele was involved in the treachery against the Hanchons. And John Hanchon had already told his adopted son that Seth Carlson was involved. But now, Riley made it clear, the commanding officer of the powerful 7th Cavalry had accepted their "Indian menace" tale—meaning it was not just Steele and his hardcase gunmen they had to fight, but the U.S. Army as well.

"I'm trying to prize out what information I can," said Riley. "I like your ma and pa. They've worked hard to make a good living and to make this valley a decent place to live. It puts blood in my eyes to see the big nabobs like Hiram Steele doing dirt on them. Corey told me all about what Steele and Carlson did to you. Tell you the truth, you had every right to stick that knife in me a few minutes ago. Though I'm damn glad you didn't!"

"Tom's got an idea," said Corey. "He's off duty today, but his superiors have got him on maneuvers in the field all around this area and further north. It's hard for him to get word to me quick when he learns something at the fort. So he says we should rig up a way for him to leave messages nearby."

Touch the Sky nodded, then briefly translated for Little Horse.

"These men we're fighting," said Touch the Sky to Corey and Riley, "aren't Steele's usual wranglers. They blacked their faces for war against my people before they ever rode into this valley."

He explained about the whiskey seller Henri Lagace and his crew of mercenaries, who had scattered after the Cheyenne raid on their mountain stronghold. Riley nodded, recognizing the name.

"That bunch is wanted for a series of murders and robberies up in the Northern Territory. Crimes they tried to pin on the Cheyennes. So some of 'em are working for Steele? That means they're safe from any law around here."

"Any white man's law," said Touch the Sky grimly. "They have killed my people. My battle axe is raised against them until death."

"Maybe," said Riley, "but you and your friend will be damn lucky to keep your hide, let alone skin anybody else. It's not just Steele's riffraff you're up against. I heard all about how Carlson made a fool of himself yesterday in front of his men, trying to put you under. As sure as hell's afire he'll be looking behind every stone and bush for you two."

He again mentioned the need for a system to leave messages. When Touch the Sky translated to Little Horse, he nodded and signaled everyone to follow him. They moved up into the trees and followed a deer run, skirting wide at one point to avoid a patch of trees which had been obliterated by a rock slide. Little Horse stopped at a leather-leaved cottonwood with a fork split deep by lightning.

"That's the gait," said Riley to Touch the Sky. "Check that fork daily for messages. And be careful 'cause Carlson's got sentries posted night and day up on Thompson's Bluff, watching the road into your pa's spread."

Touch the Sky nodded. In fact he and Little Horse had already spotted the sentries. Which meant, Touch the Sky reminded himself, that there was a good chance Hiram Steele knew his daughter had been with the Hanchons and their "savage" boy.

"I've got to make tracks now," said Riley. "But I'll be in contact."

Now Touch the Sky permitted himself to meet the young brevet officer's gaze. "Why do you risk trouble for yourself helping us?"

Riley shrugged. "Maybe it'll be turnabout someday. I got kin back East want to come out here. First we need more settlers like your ma and pa, not like Hiram Steele."

Riley and Corey returned to the camp for their horses. Touch the Sky and Little Horse worked their way cautiously down to the river, staying out of sight. The two Cheyennes stripped and bathed in the ice-cold water, then lay in the warming sun to dry. Sandpipers waded along the shore, magpies screamed, woodpeckers kept up a steady rat-a-tat from the trees overhead.

At one point, hearing the distant heave-ho cadence of boatmen, the two scrambled up the bank and hid in the thickets while a keelboat floated by. A blunderbuss was mounted on a swivel in the prow, and the deck was crowded with crates of whiskey and rifles. Though the river was full, they were traveling against the current and there was no favoring wind. Six men lined each side of the flat-bottomed boat, using long wooden poles to propel it.

"More trouble for the red man," said Little Horse.

His remark reminded both of them, again, that they were up against a ruthless enemy.

"Brother," said Little Horse, "I would speak with you."

"You know that I have ears for it."

"Just now, as you were grappling with the Bluecoat? He pushed your hair far back off your forehead and I noticed the mark. Why have you not spoken of this thing?"

Touch the Sky was silent at first, though he knew well what mark Little Horse meant: In the hair just above his left temple, buried past the hairline, was a mulberry-colored birthmark shaped like an arrowhead—the traditional mark of the Cheyenne warrior.

"Brother," insisted Little Horse, "what does this thing mean?"

Again Touch the Sky held his silence, unsure how to speak or even what to say. Would Little Horse believe him if he repeated what Arrow Keeper insisted: that Touch the Sky was the long-lost son of Running Antelope, a great young chief of the Northern Cheyennes who was killed in a Bluecoat ambush?

When Touch the Sky said nothing, Little Horse only shook his head. "The hand of Maiyun is in this thing," he said quietly. "That mark means we will face many battles. If we must die, brother, let it be after we kill these paleface devils who attacked our tribe and now attack your white clan!"

Wolf Who Hunts Smiling had always claimed that Touch the Sky was secretly a spy for the Bluecoats. And although he pretended to agree, in fact Swift Canoe had always doubted this.

He had cause enough to hate this white man's "Cheyenne." Had he not caused the death of Swift Canoe's twin brother, True Son?

So it shocked him now as, hidden with River of Winds, they watched Touch the Sky and Little Horse making medicine with a Bluecoat!

The two Cheyenne spies had missed the earlier struggle, still searching for the camp after locating Little Horse and Touch the Sky's tethered ponies. Now all they saw was an earnest discussion between Touch the Sky and the officer.

Touch the Sky translated for Little Horse, and Swift Canoe said, "Did you hear, brother? They are talking about leaving messages for each other! Touch the Sky and this murdering white dog! Wolf Who Hunts Smiling spoke the straight word all along! He is a spy!"

River of Winds, who was several winters older than Swift Canoe and far less fiery-tempered, frowned. Keeping his voice low like Swift Canoe, he said, "Do not wade in before you look, Cheyenne. We do not know what this meeting means. Firetop knows this long knife—would you deny that Firetop saved our tribe? And it was Touch the Sky who rode for him when he saved us. Why would our enemy do this thing for us? Why not let the Pawnee destroy us?"

Swift Canoe stubbornly shook his head. "Perhaps he has become their spy since then. Perhaps Firetop now works for Bluecoat gold and has turned his heart to stone toward us."

They followed as the two Indians and two whites went upridge to select the lightning-split cottonwood. Then Firetop and the Bluecoat returned to camp and rode off. The spies from Yellow Bear's camp followed their fellow Cheyennes as they cautiously worked their way down toward the river.

They hid in a deep swale while Touch the Sky and Little Horse bathed.

"Brother," said Swift Canoe, "I ask only this. Once you have seen enough to convince you Touch the Sky is a double-tongued spy, let me kill him then and there."

"What, and would you kill Little Horse too? You will not kill one without killing the other. Even if, as you claim, Touch the Sky has stained the Sacred Arrows by causing True Son's death, you have no right to punish Little Horse. He must then go before the councillors."

Swift Canoe was silent at this rebuke, resenting it but knowing the older warrior was right.

Still, there would surely come a moment when Little Horse and Touch the Sky were separated, thought Swift Canoe. The warrior wanted once and for all to end the taunts and sly remarks of other Cheyenne bucks, who had begun to mock both him and Wolf Who Hunts Smiling as empty boasters. Once his enemy was proven a spy, the tribe would honor him for killing Touch the Sky.

"As you say, brother," he said. "We will wait and watch."

Chapter Nine

The Powder always ran swift and cold early in the warm moons. Shivering, her naked, coltish body dappled with gooseflesh, Honey Eater stepped up onto the grassy bank and dried off with handfuls of willow leaves.

The biting cold of the river, and a cool sting in the early morning air, had left her teeth chattering. But she welcomed the slap to her senses after another sleepless night's vigil with her ailing father.

Well hidden behind the wall of tall rushes which marked off the women's bathing area, she slipped into her moccasins and a dress made of soft kid leather. Her wet hair was unbraided now and hung in long black tresses.

Then she lingered for a long moment, her pretty, finely sculpted face sad with the weight of her problems. Touch the Sky was gone, and her father was about to leave her too! Honey Eater could not muster the usual happiness of the snow-melting season. Instead, she felt only the haunting, hollow sadness of loss that she always felt in the Moon When the Geese Fly South when the trees were shaking off their leaves.

The first thing she noticed, when she stepped past the wall of rushes, was the Lakota camp. It was well downstream on the opposite bank. Already, as in the Cheyenne camp, smoke curled from the top-holes of the tipis. They were constructed almost exactly like those of their Cheyenne cousins. But the more modest Cheyennes included a flap over the entrance to ensure privacy.

Honey Eater welcomed the presence of Chief Sun Dance and his Lakotas. Their warriors were fierce, their ponies swift. Several Lakotas had married into Yellow Bear's tribe, and Honey Eater knew of Cheyennes living with Sun Dance's people. The two tribes would fight to the death for each other.

True, the Lakotas were here only temporarily, until their hunt began. But such reassurance was welcome now, with her father fighting for each breath. The loss of any member of the tribe brought bad medicine, of course. But a chief's passing left a tribe at its most vulnerable.

As she crossed the camp, she saw some of the old grandmothers gathering with their willow-stem baskets. They were going out this morning to gather acorns and wild peas.

She kept her eyes downcast, but she was aware that Black Elk was already awake and stirring. He sat before his tipi, plaiting a bridle out of rawhide and horsehair.

Though he too avoided glancing in her direction, she knew he saw her. And she could not help wondering: Is that new bridle for one of the horses he plans to offer as the bride-price for my love?

She lifted the flap of her tipi and saw Arrow Keeper sitting cross-legged beside her father's robes.

"Come in, little daughter," he said. "I dismissed the grandmother so that we might talk."

"I always place your words close to my heart."

"Yes, you do. And therefore I always select them carefully. Come, little Honey Eater—come look at your father."

She did. Little had changed since she left to bathe. His craggy, nut-brown face was emaciated, the flesh drawn knuckle-tight on the prominent cheekbones. His silver-white hair lay fanned out like a mane. It reminded her of the days when he wore a magnificent crow-feather war bonnet and led braves into battle shouting the war cry.

"Look at him, daughter, and remember him well. Soon, very soon now, he makes his final journey."

Arrow Keeper made the cut-off sign.

"You must be strong, little one. You have suffered terribly and will suffer more. But you must not hold this bitterness in your heart toward Touch the Sky. He has not deserted you or his tribe."

"Father, I hear your words, but how can they be true? Is he here now? Did he not ride out before the Lakota made their camp near ours?"

"He did, daughter. But love fought with duty in his heart, and he did not make his decision lightly. He rode into great danger, faces danger at this moment, to help the only mother and father he has known.

"Honey Eater, are you a Cheyenne maiden? Or are you like the cold Comanches below the Platte, who scorn clan loyalties and leave their old parents to starve in the short white days?"

Tears filmed her eyes, one lone crystal drop dripping from a lash. "You are right, Father. It is good that Touch the Sky loves his white parents enough to fight for them. But I am afraid. Afraid for him, and afraid for myself."

She didn't need to say more. It would be unseemly to speak of such things now, over the dying chief. But Honey Eater was hinting about the tribal law which declared that a marriageable maiden must live with either her father, her brother, or her husband.

Arrow Keeper nodded, his seamed face troubled. It was true that he now believed firmly in the medicine vision which had foretold Touch the Sky's greatness. But nothing in that vision told him that Touch the Sky and Honey Eater, despite their powerful love, would eventually celebrate the squaw-taking ceremony. Black Elk was a fierce warrior, older than Touch the Sky and far richer in the spoils of battle. He was also the tribe's war chief.

"I understand your fear, daughter," Arrow Keeper finally said. "But you must be prepared to do your duty. You cannot defy the will of the tribe. A chief's daughter has a special obligation."

She was about to reply when old Yellow Bear abruptly sat up, eyes wide open and blazing, and called her name!

The shock of it froze both Honey Eater and Arrow Keeper. The chief, clearly in a trance though his eyes were wide open, stared only at his daughter. He seemed unaware of Arrow Keeper's presence.

"Honey Eater," said his gravelly, tired voice, "the tall young stranger is meant to be a chief. But his path will be hard and his enemies many. Love him, my little daughter, but hold these words close to your heart.

"Happiness is a short, warm moment, and suffering is a long, cold night. The red nations have tasted their greatest glory. From now on the red man runs from death alongside his brother the buffalo. This tall young stranger will be the last of the great Cheyenne war chiefs. Behind him the Shaiyena people will raise their battle cry in one last, great victory.

"I love you, Honey Eater. You have always been the soul of this old warrior's medicine bag. Now I go to join your mother. Do not weep for me, daughter. Bring children into this world, and sing to them about their grandfather and the old ways."

Yellow Bear collapsed, sucked in a long, rattling breath, then sang the death song in a weak but clear voice:

Nothing lives long,
Only the earth and the mountains.

The next moment the chief died, his face weary but at peace.

Despite his request, Honey Eater burst into sobs, a knife point of grief twisting deep inside her.

Arrow Keeper still sat motionless, profoundly moved. Hovering near death, Yellow Bear too had experienced the vision of Touch the Sky's greatness. But now Honey Eater's father was gone, and Touch the Sky had few in the tribe to speak up for him. His present battle with the palefaces was not his only problem. If the hapless youth did not return soon, he would lose the happiness of his life to Black Elk.

And even if he did return in time, Black Elk would never surrender her without a fight to the death.

But for now ancient custom took over. Arrow Keeper stepped outside and sent a young boy running to fetch the camp crier. His face solemn at the news of Yellow Bear's death, the brave swung onto his pony. He raced up and down the camp, crying at the top of his lungs:

"Our chief has crossed over! Our chief has crossed over!"

The keening wail of the mourners soon filled the camp. Downriver, the overheard cry was likewise being spread by the Lakotas, for whom this was also a terrible and solemn occasion. But Honey Eater dried her eyes and touched her father's dead face in a gesture of farewell.

Now the call of tribal duty was strong in her. There would be many things to do. Of course, at a time like this, it was usual for one of the honored grandmothers to prepare a chief for his final journey. But now she must take charge and show she was strong—was she not the proud daughter of a great chief?

His body must be washed and dressed, and he would need new moccasins for his long journey to the Land of Ghosts. She hurried outside, knowing she must greet the mourners as they visited their dead chief.

Black Elk was among the first who were heading toward the tipi. *Hurry, Touch the Sky,* she thought. *Hurry! I am alone now!*

Wolf Who Hunts Smiling was a warrior now. Despite his youth, he was entrusted with the important task of training the young bucks in the arts of Cheyenne warfare.

Nonetheless, a certain story had made the rounds at Yellow Bear's camp. It was well known that, at the very moment they were both needed to protect their war chief from white bullets, Wolf Who Hunts Smiling and Touch the Sky had instead fought each other for the honor of the first kill. None of the bucks was foolish enough to mention this in front of Wolf Who Hunts Smiling. But his ears, like his furtive eyes, missed nothing—he had heard them speak of this thing, scorn in their voices.

Now, as he led a party of six young bucks on a hunting trip near the Little Bighorn River, his mind raced for ways to unite the warriors in training behind him. Wolf Who Hunts Smiling admired his cousin Black Elk greatly. But Black Elk's heart was too soft and womanly toward this white man's dog who dared take the Cheyenne name Touch the Sky. Wolf Who Hunts Smiling had watched the Bluecoats turn his own father into raw, shredded meat when his body absorbed the full impact of a canister shell. Black Elk was indeed strong and brave. But his head and heart were soft toward the white dogs who must be driven from the red man's land!

They were hunting with bows only. Only now was the tribe starting to accumulate new beaver pelts for trade. The hunters and warriors were without ammunition and gun patches and black powder. So Wolf Who Hunts Smiling ordered his subordinates to remain silent and downwind when they spotted a black bear ahead beside the game trail. Arrows would only enrage it for the kill. They let it roll aside a log to get at the beetles beneath it before they rode on.

Good meat was scarce and the racks back at Yellow Bear's camp almost empty. There were some stringy elk in the foothills, and the Arapahoes reported small buffalo herds between the Black Hills and the Niobrara River. But most of the big herds were running well to the north, far north of the Marias River. Already they sensed that the old runs to the south had become trails of senseless slaughter, thanks to the white men and their .53-caliber buffalo balls.

"Little brothers!" said Wolf Who Hunts Smiling when they stopped to water their ponies. "The tribe needs meat. Keep your eyes sharp for a fat mule deer or antelope! He who sinks first arrow eats the liver!"

That night they camped in a cedar brake near the Little Bighorn. All day long Wolf Who Hunts Smiling had been plagued by thoughts of Touch the Sky. Every day longer that he was alive added fresh humiliation and torment to the shame Wolf Who Hunts Smiling already felt. He had vowed to kill this capable young warrior when Touch the Sky was still untrained in the killing ways. Now his boast was proving difficult to carry out.

"Cheyenne bucks," said Wolf Who Hunts Smiling while the embers still glowed bright, "there is nothing more dangerous to a tribe than an Indian turncoat!

"You know already that River of Winds and Swift Canoe have been sent into long-knife territory. They have gone for the purpose of finally proving that Touch the Sky is a double-tongued spy. Perhaps Little Horse too plays the fox with his own people. More than one red man has killed a brother in his sleep for white man's gold or strong water."

Wolf Who Hunts Smiling paused, savoring the taste of power over these young bucks who would become the tribe's future warriors. He must be careful. Though their lives were remote from those of Yellow Bear, Arrow Keeper, and the other elders with 60 and more winters behind them, they respected young warriors like Black Elk, their war chief.

"Little brothers, I do not speak in a wolf bark against any of the Headmen. But when you ask among yourselves why has this dangerous spy been permitted to live among us, look to the councillors and your medicine man and your chief. This thing has not happened because they do not love their tribe. It is because they are soft and sentimental with old age, like old women who recall their dead children and openly weep.

"A warrior must be a tree covered with hard bark! Do you not observe how the red men live who lie down like dogs for the long knives? The paleface is our sworn enemy, and we must scatter his bones across the plains and prairies, throughout the mountains and the valleys! We can trust no one who would make medicine with the white men, no one who would desert his red tribe and ride to fight battles for those who take our land

and kill our people! A Cheyenne cannot place anything before his duty to his tribe. I tell you now this Touch the Sky is not one of us, and even now he is lending strength to our enemies!"

Chapter Ten

Two sleeps passed without trouble after the horse-scattering incident. While their sister the sun made her journey through the sky, Touch the Sky and Little Horse moved with ease around the perimeter of the Hanchon spread. Several times they spotted Steele's riders on Hanchon land, apparently checking on the location of the mustang herds. The two Cheyennes stuck to the trees and thickets, made quick time through the many cutbanks and coulees. Their experience in concealment served them well now.

When their uncle the moon owned the sky, they built a small cedar and willow fire, smothering it frequently to produce smoke for scenting their clothing and moccasins. Winds changed unpredictably near the river, and mustangs unused to the smell of Indians might well stampede when they didn't want them to, giving them away.

Under cover of darkness they also visited the house. Sarah Hanchon insisted on serving them hot food, and to Touch the Sky's astonishment Little Horse devoured everything with intense pleasure. Once, when she heaped a third helping of biscuits and honey on Little Horse's plate, Touch the Sky saw his friend briefly glance at Sarah Hanchon and meet her eyes with respectful gratitude. Around John Hanchon too Little Horse was at ease. Only when Wade McKenna was present did Little Horse withdraw into himself and cast his eyes down at one unvarying spot on the floor.

"All the mustangs you two scattered are back in the summer meadow," said John Hanchon. He was cleaning the Henry, and it was broken open before him on the oilcloth-covered deal table in the kitchen. "They never left our land, so it was no trouble pointing them. Woody won't be on his feet for days yet, and it's no good to me when he is because he quit. He's the second one in as many days. Hell, the next man that demands his wages in full will have to take it in hay and grass."

Despite the forced jocularity of his remark, Hanchon showed his concern in the deepening network of lines around his eyes and mouth. He was now left with only five wranglers and Wade McKenna. Not only was defending his property a problem—soon he might not even be able to work it.

Luckily he had recently come into some hard cash providing 30 saddle-broke horses for a keelboat company, and they needed 30 more again in a month. Still, he was unable to seek new business so long as he was tied up in fighting for his very survival.

Touch the Sky read the worry in his parents' faces, and again felt hatred for Steele and every other greedy white man who thought the green earth and all her creatures belonged to them to buy and sell. Thinking of the sentry, he asked his mother if she'd heard any more from Kristen Steele. But Sarah only bit her lower lip and frowned, answering that she'd heard nothing. She was worried about the same question that troubled Touch the Sky: Did Hiram know she'd come out here again against his orders?

On that second night, at Sarah's insistence, the two Cheyennes filled their legging sashes with cold biscuits and dried fruit and jerked beef. Early the next morning, while Little Horse went to check on their ponies, Touch the Sky went upridge and into the trees. He followed the deer run until he reached the lightning-split cottonwood. He had checked it every morning since he and Riley agreed to use it for messages.

This time, when his hand groped deep into the charred opening, his fingers encountered a folded scrap of paper.

Move your camp out of this area, Riley had written. *Carlson due through this area soon searching for you. Suggest you camp closer to Steele's property. But keep checking this spot for messages.*

They took the Bluecoat's advice. That night, aided by a moonless, cloudy sky, they rode due west until they reached a hogback ridge which bordered Steele's spread. From there they could keep an eye on his riders yet be within a short ride of the Hanchon property.

They camped well below the steep crest of the hogback, selecting a thickly wooded hollow. They built a crude brush lean-to for protection from rain. Unfortunately, there wasn't much forage available for the ponies, and it was necessary to occasionally move them about to new patches of graze, risking exposure from the main yard below.

Despite all the precaution of this move, however, the two Cheyennes very nearly rode square into death.

It was the second day after their move to the new camp. Avoiding the trail and riding high along the ridge, Touch the Sky and Little Horse rode back to their old campsite to check for messages in the cottonwood. The fork was empty. They had just swung onto their ponies and pointed them back toward Steele's property when they saw a Bluecoat pony squad advancing toward their position from below the ridge.

The arrogant Seth Carlson led them! Touch the Sky realized this was the patrol Riley had warned them about—the patrol sent to search them out like holed-up rats.

"Brother!" said Touch the Sky. "It is useless to try outrunning the pony soldiers. The trees on this ridge are our only cover, but they grow too close together for hard, fast riding."

Little Horse nodded. "And they would hear the sounds of hard riding. We must take cover."

Concealing their ponies presented the immediate problem. By now the Bluecoats were almost within hailing distance of the tree line. At a command from Carlson they formed up at close intervals, only a few yards between each trooper.

"Brother," said Little Horse, "this is a search party, not just a patrol riding through. These palefaces mean to turn over every leaf!"

Touch the Sky's mouth was a grim, determined slit. He nodded.

"We must hide well or be prepared to sing the death song," he said. "Quickly, strip the bridle and blanket from your pony! We must turn her loose on the far side of the trees. If the soldiers spot her, we can only hope they do not recognize her. Perhaps they will mistake her for a stray mustang from one of the spreads."

Little Horse stripped the powerful little chestnut. They hoped the Bluecoats would not ride close enough to spot the handprint he had made with claybank war paint on the pony's left front forequarter, the Cheyenne way of marking a pony's owner.

Little Horse led the chestnut further up the ridge and turned her loose to graze on the opposite side of the tree line. Touch the Sky knew this ruse was too risky for his own dun. Carlson had gotten too long and close a look at her when he charged Touch the Sky. But this pony had been especially trained by Arrow Keeper.

Quickly, Touch the Sky led her to a patch of open ground which appeared worthless for hiding. He hoped the patrol would bypass it in favor of denser undergrowth.

Touch the Sky made a snorting noise like a horse drinking. Immediately, the dun lay down flat on her side, head down.

The Bluecoat patrol was only about 30 yards from the tree line, and closing steadily, by the time Touch the Sky and Little Horse finished covering the dun with fallen leaves and branches. From a short distance off there appeared to be only a small hummock rising from the ridge.

"Quickly!" said Little Horse. "There is a stream

close by. I saw a place where we might hide when I was leading my pony out. But it means we must risk leaving the rifles here with your pony."

"Stay at close intervals!" they heard Carlson shout behind them. "Dismount at the tree line and tether your horses. Then fix bayonets. We'll move through the trees on foot. Search thoroughly, and probe your steel into that brush! These are dangerous bucks, so shoot on sight!"

The two Cheyennes reached the stream and waded through it, crossing on the opposite bank toward a huge tree. Its huge, shaggy network of roots had been exposed where the stream had eaten away the dirt beneath it. This left a slight hollow tucked up under the bank of the stream.

The chilly water was dark with spring soil runoff. They ducked under and, one at a time, helping each other, squeezed through the narrow opening beneath the tree roots. They were barely able to secrete their heads and shoulders into the slight opening, the rest of their bodies hidden by the murky water.

At first they could hear nothing but the steady rush of the water all around them. But their keen ears soon detected the sounds of the thorough search as they grew steadily louder. Heavy leather boots stomped through the undergrowth, bayonets sliced into the bushes and brambles and deadfalls.

"Brother," said Little Horse, speaking directly into his friend's ear in a voice just above a whisper, "our enemy is upon us! My knife is in my hand, and I see yours is ready also. If we are meant to die, let it be like *warriors,* right here, right now, with the death song on our lips and our blades seeking warm vitals! I swear to you I will fall on my own knife before I let them take me prisoner!"

"I swear this thing to you too. By the four directions, I swear they will never lock you in the soldier house while I have breath in me."

They fell silent as the sounds of searching grew closer. Heavy, uneven splashes told them soldiers had entered the stream nearby.

"You, Davis!" shouted Carlson's voice, so close that Touch the Sky jerked in surprise. "Afraid to get your feet wet, soldier? Check up under that tree. They might have a cache there."

More splashing, much nearer now. Touch the Sky tried to pull as much of his body as possible up under the bank. After what seemed an unbearably long time, the splashing ceased as the Bluecoat left the water. Touch the Sky expelled a long sigh of relief.

The next moment, a sharp bayonet with a blood gutter tooled into it just missed his left eye by inches when it probed through the thin layer of dirt above them.

Another thrust, another, each further away from his face.

The soldier added a fourth and final jab, this one slicing deep through Little Horse's right shoulder on its way back out.

Little Horse hissed at the sudden, fiery pain which took him by surprise, but otherwise made no sound or movement to give them away. A minute later they heard the searching noises grow dimmer again as the squad advanced toward the other side of the tree line.

They knew they must wait for the Bluecoats to return and remount, moving further downridge. Little Horse ducked lower in the cold water, slowing the loss of blood from his wound.

After the patrol had finally moved further east, the fugitives gratefully escaped from the cramped hiding place. Touch the Sky retrieved their weapons and the obedient dun and quickly hobbled her before he led Little Horse's pony back into the trees. Then he gouged out balsam sap and packed it into his friend's wound before binding it with soft strips of red willow bark.

"The Bluecoat officer is more determined than I thought," said Touch the Sky. "This wound is clean, though it has sliced deep. Your arm will be stiff."

"I can still hold this weapon," Little Horse said, hoisting the scattergun to prove his words. "And good thing. After this thing today, I see that battles are coming."

A sharp lance of guilt passed through Touch the Sky. He had not told his friend exactly why the Bluecoat officer was so determined. He had not explained that Carlson was not just tracking down two renegade Cheyennes—that in fact he was after one particular Cheyenne who'd had the gall to kiss a white woman. Was it fair that he place his friend's life in danger over such a personal battle?

As they cautiously rode back to their camp, Touch the Sky tried briefly to speak of this. But Little Horse silenced him.

"Brother, if a snake crawls into my tipi, I do not ask whether it is seeking food or warmth. I know only that a snake is in my tipi. It does not matter to me why this Bluecoat seeks to put you under. All these things you tell me lead to one truth which you may place in your sash: Your greatest crime is being a Cheyenne!"

He spoke straight-arrow, and Touch the Sky fell silent. Their enemies surrounded them, and now it was time to forget words and listen to the language of nature. They had fooled the Bluecoats today, true. But neither Cheyenne felt like boasting or celebrating their great skill, as warriors often do after a victory.

The Bluecoats would be back. And even now, with each step their ponies took, they grew closer to Hiram Steele's property and a second enemy even more ruthless than the Bluecoats.

Chapter Eleven

"Truth to tell," said Abe Winslow, "I ain't seed hide nor hair of these red varmints that got you all consternated."

"They're out there," said Hiram Steele. "Sure as gumption, they're out there. That was no bear that spooked those mustangs the other night."

"By hell, it sounded pure-dee bear, and this hoss has let daylight into more than one. You yourself say that shavetail lieutenant and his men have combed this area and can't find sign of them."

"There's only two," said Steele. "That makes it easier to hide."

Winslow absently scratched at his pockmarked face. He stood just inside the door of Steele's house, slouched beaver in his hand. Removing his hat was not a mark of respect toward Steele. It was nervousness—the only solid buildings the former mountain man turned outlaw had been inside in 20 years were trading posts and jail-houses.

"Two," said Winslow. "And what tribe did you say they was?"

"I didn't, but it's Cheyenne."

This news did not set well with Winslow. Frowning, he said, "You didn't say nothing about no Cheyennes when we talked terms."

"They weren't around then."

"Well, they are now. And I'll tell you straight from the shoulder, me and my men have already had our bellyful of fighting Cheyennes."

"No need to get skittish," said Steele. "There's only two of them, and they've barely got their growth."

This information made Winslow cock his head with sudden interest. "Young bucks, you say?"

"Yes, why?"

Winslow was silent for several moments, lost in reflection. "Young, you say. What do they look like?"

Something in the hardcase's tone alerted Steele. The rancher shrugged his beefy shoulders. "Look like? Hell, all Indians look alike to me."

"Then you ain't never stood a Pawnee next to a Flathead! Is one of the bucks tall for an Indian?"

Steele's eyes cut impatiently away. "The hell, you think I measure every renegade that rides through this valley?"

Winslow sniffed a rat here. He despised Hiram Steele and all other men, farmers or ranchers, who pounded their stake in one spot and worked it for life. But money talks and bullshit walks, was Winslow's motto, and Steele paid up every week in gold nuggets.

Still, this talk about young Cheyenne bucks cankered at him. He had seen what a handful of them did to Henri Lagace's mountain stronghold, from which Winslow had been lucky to escape with his topknot still attached.

"I'll tell you straight right now," he said. "When the men find out we're huggin' with Cheyennes, they'll want more money."

"Show me their dead bodies, and there'll be more money. Plenty more."

Steele walked to the front window and pushed the curtain aside. Beyond the main yard, several of his regular hands were erecting a big new pole corral.

"Whether it's bears or Indians," said Steele, "this next raid won't be stopped. I'll see to that. And when I set my mind to something, you can call it as good as done."

Only one sleep after they avoided the Bluecoat search party, the two Cheyennes spotted new signs of possible trouble.

A new pole corral was going up, yet there was no sign that Steele's wranglers were planning to ride out after wild mustangs. A corral this large could only mean that Steele planned to acquire a large number of horses soon.

"Steele's fed up with the penny-ante game," said John Hanchon that night when Touch the Sky and Little Horse visited the house and told him about the new corral. "He's going to raise the stakes sky high this next time, and drive us out. That corral is for my horses—there's not another good herd of wild mustangs between here and the Niobrara River, and Steele knows that."

Later, in the shelter of their brush lean-to, Touch the Sky lay on his back and watched the stars through the entrance hole. He thought again about the worry lines permanently etched into his parents' faces. And he thought about Hiram Steele, who drove him out of this territory for no other crime than being an Indian.

"Brother," he said to Little Horse in the cool darkness, "I am weary of always waiting for our enemy to act before we know their plans. This new corral, I must learn their plans for it."

"I have ears for this," said Little Horse. "But how? Will you turn into a bird and fly among them, listening?"

"Only Arrow Keeper's big medicine might turn me into a bird. But yes, I will go among them and listen."

He heard Little Horse sit up in his robe. His voice was low with seriousness when he said, "Brother, have you gone Wendigo? They will spit you and roast you over the embers."

"I will sneak up on the lodge where the men sleep," said Touch the Sky. "Whites always foolishly wag their tongues. Perhaps I will learn more about this corral, learn when and how they will attack my father's ranch. Black Elk was right, a warrior must always own the element of surprise."

Little Horse was silent for many heartbeats. Touch the Sky was right about surprise, of course. But this was a dangerous move, this plan to enter the vipers' nest.

"I agree," Little Horse finally said. "But I must go with you."

"I have no ears for this talk! But think, it is I who understand the paleface tongue. It will be easier for one to sneak in than two."

"It is no use, brother. You will reverse the wind

before you change Little Horse's mind. I go with you. Now let us talk about this thing."

Touch the Sky could tell, from his friend's tone, that he meant what he said. So the two friends counseled in earnest, glad at last for this clear course of action.

Little Horse reminded him: This mission would take place after the fall of darkness, that eternal foe of the Cheyennes. This was bad medicine. It meant they could not kill nor even attack an enemy without staining the tribe's sacred Medicine Arrows forever. Therefore, he argued, they must prepare an elaborate defense tomorrow, during the day. A defense designed to delay their enemies, should they be forced to flee, without requiring them to actually fight except as a last resort.

The next morning they selected a shallow, rocky basin as their emergency escape route. It lay directly behind the bunkhouse, separated from the pine log building by a meadow and a line of low hills. That afternoon a sudden thunder squall darkened the area and sent all the hands seeking shelter. The Cheyennes took advantage of the bad weather to prepare their escape. They worked well into the evening, chewing on jerked beef and dried plums to ease the gnawing in their bellies.

Touch the Sky had already studied the bunkhouse carefully, one evening when he and Little Horse had sneaked close to the main yard to estimate the number of men working for Steele. He knew that there was one window, just around the front corner from the doorway. It was covered with oiled paper, but one corner had torn out leaving an opening the size of a fist.

"I will be able to hear them," said Touch the

Sky as they prepared to approach the yard. "But I will be exposed in the moonlight on a side the sentry can see clearly. You must remain back behind near the corral as my lookout. If the sentry approaches, sound the owl hoot."

Little Horse agreed in a nod. Their danger was extreme because they had both decided to leave all weapons except their throwing axes back at camp as a gesture of assurance to Maiyun, the Good Supernatural, that they would not attack after dark as did the treacherous Pawnees. Their axes would be hidden at the edge of the rocky basin. If trapped or captured before they reached the basin, they had no defense.

Although the cream-colored moonlight exposed them, it also made for an easy journey on foot down from their campsite to the outlying pastures of the Steele spread. The two Cheyennes waited for occasional scuds of clouds to sweep in front of the moon. Then they would race closer to the bunkhouse, staying low to the ground and keeping their faces down as much as possible to cut reflection or glare from their eyes.

At the far corner of the last corral, Touch the Sky gripped his friend's arm and squeezed it. Little Horse nodded. For a long moment, crouched in the shadow of the corral poles, they felt united in their common goal of defeating their enemy. Every sense was alive, alert, and the copper taste of fear was mixed with the sweet, thrilling scent of victory for their people.

"Wait here, brother," whispered Little Horse. "I hear the sentry."

The smaller Cheyenne's keen ears proved right again. It was a full ten heartbeats before Touch the Sky heard the wrangler's mount approaching from the opposite side of the yard. The man made a pass around the bunkhouse and the main house, throwing a long, eerie shadow in the stark moonlight. Then he swung out toward the outlying sheds and pens.

"Slide easy like that paleface's shadow," said Little Horse, "and leave one ear listening for the owl, brother! And remember, you carry no weapons!"

Touch the Sky searched the yard one final time. Then he rose in a crouch and crossed the open expanse between the corral and the corner of the bunkhouse. He flattened himself against the building and inched closer to the opening in the oiled paper. A yellow beam of lantern light shot out like a stray shaft of sunlight.

He could hear the mournful twang of a Jew's harp. Snatches of conversation escaped through the hole like bugs.

"God strike me dead now if it ain't the truth! I did so meet the Queen of England!"

"Why prove up a homestead jist to see the gum 'ment boys give it all back to the Innuns?"

"You ask *this* white nigger, I won't poke no redheaded woman. They got a bush down there like a prickly pear."

Touch the Sky was about to find a more comfortable position, ready to settle in for a long wait. At that moment a hound trotted around the corner and spotted him.

A growl bubbled low in its throat.

The next moment it began a furious barking.

"The hell?" shouted somebody inside the bunkhouse. "Who goes out there?"

The door banged open and Touch the Sky sprang toward the corral.

"Fly like the wind, brother!" he said to Little Horse.

"Over there by the corral!" a man shouted. "Two of 'em, see?"

A couple of men had grabbed weapons as they ran outside. They opened fire. Slugs whanged past the Cheyennes' ears. Several men gave chase on foot while others raced for their stalled horses.

"Do not run in a straight line, brother!" said Little Horse. "It makes an easy target!"

They zigzagged across the open meadow and into the low hills, bullets nipping at their heels all the way. Now they could hear the ominous pounding of shod hooves as the first mounted wranglers gave chase.

Touch the Sky looked over his shoulder and recognized the sentry leading the group. He was closing fast, not bothering to draw his sidearm. Clearly he meant to move into killing range first before he wasted a cap.

They could hear their enemies' horses snorting now. They put on a final burst of speed and reached the edge of the rock-strewn basin.

Touch the Sky was first to reach the boulder behind which they'd stashed their axes. The sentry gave sharp spur to his mount, surging even closer as the two Cheyennes stopped to face him.

"No blood!" Little Horse shouted as Touch the Sky cocked his arm. The tall Cheyenne unleashed the double-bladed throwing axe. It spun end over end and sliced clean through one of the latigos of the sentry's saddle. The cinch immediately broke and the saddle slid quickly around, tossing the rider clear.

"Quickly!" said Touch the Sky. "Remember the route!"

They raced along the trail they had prepared earlier. Now bullets ricocheted from boulders as more riders closed in.

Suddenly, a horse crashed to the ground, its legs entwined in leather ropes the Cheyennes had strung there earlier.

Another rider bore down on them, close enough now to draw steel. He was drawing a bead on Touch the Sky's back when he raised one hand to swipe at an obstructing branch.

There was a noise like a whip cracking as his swipe released the powerfully bent branch the Cheyennes had rigged earlier. The force easily lifted him from the saddle and knocked him off his horse backwards. His spine snapped like old wood when he landed square on a jagged-edged boulder.

Enough men had gone down to slow the charge to a standstill. The two Cheyennes took refuge in a prearranged spot, a narrow cleft between one wall of the basin and a huge slab of slate.

"All right, men!" said Winslow's gravelly voice. "Steele was right after all! We got Cheyennes on the warpath agin us! That's enough for tonight. Round up the horses and tend to the wounded."

"What about Myers?" said one of the men. "His back is snapped clean. He's gone beaver."

The well-hidden Cheyenne warriors watched, in the stark light of the moon, as Winslow walked back to the spot where the wrangler named Myers had fallen. Without a word he drew his pistol and put a bullet in the man's brain.

"Bury him tomorrow," he said, "when you can see what the hell you're doing. And from now on, keep your weapons to hand. We got us some Cheyennes to kill!"

From the edge of the basin, well secreted in a dense thicket, Swift Canoe and River of Winds watched the drama between the whites and their fellow Cheyennes.

Several sleeps earlier, they had spied on Touch the Sky as he found the message from the Bluecoat in the cottonwood tree. Clearly he followed the pony soldier's orders. Immediately after finding the white man's talking paper, he and Little Horse had moved their camp closer to this second mustang spread.

Then, only one sleep earlier, Swift Canoe and River of Winds had followed the two friends as they again checked for messages in the tree. They had run away as soon as they spotted the Bluecoat patrol. Thus, they saw nothing that occurred between the white butchers and their fellow Cheyennes. But Swift Canoe had concluded that the soldiers were coming to meet with Touch the Sky and Little Horse.

River of Winds said nothing to his companion, who was already like a dog in the hot moon in his thirst for blood. But secretly he suspected that Swift Canoe was right.

"Brother," said Swift Canoe now, having watched wordlessly as the paleface coolly shot his wounded companion like a lame horse. "I have thought long over this thing. I have heard stories from warriors whom I trust, warriors who speak one way always. They say that the long knives often secretly attack their own people. This way they blame some enemy and profit from the spoils of war."

River of Winds was silent. But he too wondered the same thing Swift Canoe had come to accept as truth: Did this explain the apparent meeting yesterday between the Cheyennes and the Blue-coats? Had Touch the Sky and Little Horse agreed to make war against white settlers to create the appearance that Cheyennes were raiding away from their hunting grounds?

"Anything is possible," said River of Winds. "These stories you have heard from the warriors, they are true. But this does not prove that Touch the Sky and Little Horse are spies."

"I can tell from your voice, brother, that your own heart does not believe your words. These two are dogs for the white soldier who leaves talking papers in the tree! They not only sell the secrets of Yellow Bear's tribe to their enemy. They turn a powerful foe against the entire Cheyenne nation!"

"Anything is possible. We must report to the council soon. Until then, I think with my eyes and ears and nose and not with my head," said River of Winds.

"Brother, you have seen more battles and have more winters behind you than I. But sometimes you think too much with your heart too. You will have your proof, and soon. These two bucks learned the art of warfare from Black Elk. Look below and see how well they learned! But brother, even the blind buffalo can scent a wolf! How can your keen eyes not see it? These two Cheyennes are turncoats!"

Chapter Twelve

"The tribe is not content," Arrow Keeper said to the councillors and warriors. "Our chief has finally crossed over in peace, and this is a good thing. But the tribe is unhappy."

The old medicine man sat near the center pole of the council lodge, his red Hudson's Bay blanket drawn tight around his shoulders. Funeral rites for Yellow Bear were over. Now he rested high on a scaffold in a secret forest known only to the Cheyennes.

This council had been called to discuss the future of the tribe and the upcoming chief-renewal ceremony. The chief-renewal could not be held until all far-flung members of the tribe, now visiting with distant clans, could be summoned by word-bringers.

"The tribe is unhappy," said Arrow Keeper, "and I understand this thing. Good meat is scarce. Our annual Spring Dance has been delayed. We have not had our usual gathering to visit with distant clans after the long winter's isolation. We have not prayed to the Arrows and thanked the Great Spirit for these warm moons."

The old men nodded their agreement.

"Now our chief has crossed over, and we must accomplish these neglected things. The first step belongs to the Headmen. They must decide on an acting peace chief until the renewal ceremony."

Black Elk immediately rose. His long war bonnet held one eagle-tail feather for each time he'd counted coup. The crudely sewn-on flap of his dead ear gave him an especially ferocious expression.

"Fathers and brothers! I am your war chief. You have smoked the common pipe with me many times. May Black Elk die of the yellow vomit if he ever hides in his tipi while his tribe is on the warpath!

"Headmen, hear my words! Even now Arrow Keeper acts as our peace chief. He is a blooded warrior who has strewn the bones of his enemies on many battlefields! His wisdom is vast like the plains, his medicine strong as the grizzly! Be wise, Headmen, and call on Arrow Keeper to remain as our peace chief until the renewal ceremony!"

This was greeted with an instant shout of approval from both the warriors and the Headmen. The Headmen did not bother voting with their stones. A quick voice vote confirmed unanimous support for the old shaman.

"The tribe has spoken with one voice," said Arrow Keeper, "and I will obey. My first unpleasant duty is to remind all of you that the Lakotas soon leave on their hunt. I have received word from Arapaho runners that Pawnees are on the move north from their hunting grounds below the Weeping Woman River. We must take steps to fortify our camp and strengthen the outlying guard."

His last words were directed toward Black Elk. That warrior now said, "All braves must ready their battle rigs and keep them ready."

He turned toward Wolf Who Hunts Smiling.

"Cousin, you must train the junior warriors as quickly as possible! Soon we will have enough beaver pelts to take to the trading post at Red Shale. Then we will have ammunition."

Wolf Who Hunts Smiling nodded. His furtive dark eyes were ablaze now with the sense of his own importance. "My warriors will stand and hold when the battle cry sounds!" he said. "Can this be said for Touch the Sky and Little Horse? Now, when the tribe needs every warrior, where are they?"

Wolf Who Hunts Smiling had recently been speaking with several of the younger warriors, convincing them of the need to protect the tribe from outsiders in spite of the blindness of some of the elders. Now a few of them shouted their approval of his words.

"We are not here to discuss Touch the Sky," said Arrow Keeper coldly. "River of Winds and Swift Canoe will make their first report soon enough."

"It is never too soon, Father, to expose a turncoat! The sooner we kill these two-faced Cheyennes, the safer our tribe!"

This too was greeted with a chorus of shouts. Now, for the first time, anger glimmered in Arrow Keeper's tired old eyes. He surprised everyone by rising nimbly and suddenly unfolding a coyote fur pouch he had been hiding behind his blanket.

The lodge fell as silent as the forest where they placed their dead. Everyone knew what was in that pouch.

Arrow Keeper, his gnarled old hands never once trembling, unwrapped four stone-tipped arrows. Their shafts were dyed with bright blue and yellow stripes and fletched with scarlet feathers.

Arrow Keeper walked close to Wolf Who Hunts Smiling and thrust the arrows toward his face.

"Do you see these arrows, bloodthirsty Cheyenne buck? *These* are the sacred Medicine Arrows which you and all other warriors have sworn, with your life, to keep forever sweet and clean! And now, in the presence of the Arrows, will you speak boldly of shedding the blood of your own?"

Arrow Keeper's voice was brittle with anger and disappointment. Wolf Who Hunts Smiling was shamed. A hot flush crept up his neck and into his face as he saw all the warriors and Headmen staring at him, their grim faces sharing in Arrow Keeper's disapproval.

"But Father! Hear my words."

"Silence, cousin!" commanded Black Elk. "Your chief has spoken. Do not further sully our Arrows with your unmanly disrespect!"

Wolf Who Hunts Smiling obediently closed his mouth and sat down on the robe-covered floor of the lodge. But anger seethed inside of him. How he hated this tall Cheyenne stranger who always managed to make him look like a fool—even when he wasn't present!

"Wake up, niece! Must you always be dreaming?"

With a guilty start, Honey Eater forced her thoughts back to the present. The beadwork shawl she was supposed to be working on lay untouched in her lap. Her aunt, Sharp Nosed Woman, stared at her with an impatient frown.

"I am sorry, Aunt. Did you speak?"

Sharp Nosed Woman shook her head and muttered something under her breath. She was the sister of Honey Eater's dead mother, Singing Woman, who had been shot dead by Pawnees before Honey Eater's eyes.

Sharp Nosed Woman was a middle-aged widow who had lost her brave in the same attack which killed her sister. Honey Eater was required by tribal law, now that her father was gone, to live with her closest female relative until she married. Sharp Nosed Woman loved her niece. But she was a no-nonsense, practical woman who could not understand why girls would wear flowers in their hair or love a warrior who had nothing but his breechclout to his name.

"Yes, stone ears, I did speak! I asked if you are prepared to send an answer to Black Elk yet."

Honey Eater said nothing, though her pretty face mirrored her anguish and grief and confusion. She still wore the black shawl of mourning, and already Black Elk had sent the gift of horses!

"Niece, have you eaten strong mushrooms? Or did the Great Spirit grant you much beauty and the sense of a rabbit to go with it? You must marry! And none better than Black Elk. True, his dead ear is unpleasant to behold. But this is a small thing."

"I am not troubled by his ear," Honey Eater told her aunt impatiently. "Black Elk received that hurt defending his tribe. I would gladly marry a brave with ten times this many wounds, if in my heart I loved him."

"Loved him? Well, and have you looked at the goods piled outside of this tipi? *I* could love a buck capable of providing me with these things. Indeed, niece, I loved one who provided much less. And even *he* was a comfort on cold nights."

Sharp Nosed Woman smiled as she enjoyed some private memory. Then she made the cut-off sign, which one did when speaking of the dead.

"Your aunt did not marry so wisely as your mother. Do not play the fox with me, little one. Everyone in the tribe knows you love Touch the Sky. True, he is pleasing to look at. But do you see meat racks behind his tipi? How many blankets does he own?"

"How could he own anything?" said Honey Eater bitterly. "He has spent all of his time defending his life from enemies within his own tribe!"

"Is this a wise thing, loving a man with so many enemies?"

Before Honey Eater could reply, her name was shouted outside the tipi.

She recognized Black Elk's voice and realized the council must be over. She felt her throat constricting at the prospect of facing him. Honey Eater rose and crossed to the entrance flap, lifting it aside and stepping outside.

"Honey Eater," said Black Elk, one hand indicating the travois piled high with goods which lay near the tipi. By custom, no one could touch it until Black Elk had received his reply. "This is only a portion of the bride-price which I offer to your clan. The horses have already been selected, and I have made new bridles for all. Will you give me my answer now?"

Honey Eater had practiced for this moment. Now, eyes respectfully downcast, her voice pleasant but determined, she said, "Black Elk, I am a Cheyenne maiden. I know my duty to my tribe. I know also the respect due to so great a warrior as you. But I cannot give you this answer. Not yet."

"Why?" demanded Black Elk. "True, Yellow Bear's final journey has left you sad, and you need time to heal this grief. But Honey Eater, only think! I am not asking you to perform the ceremony right away, only to pledge your love to me. I want to hear the crier racing through our camp, telling all that we will marry! Tell me yes now."

She shook her head. "I cannot. Not until—not until River of Winds and Swift Canoe have reported."

"What?" Black Elk's eyes were fierce with jealous anger. "So you can learn about your tall young brave? Learn if he has been hurt or killed fighting for those who would kill all Indians like lice?"

"Black Elk, I do not have two hearts," Honey Eater said gently. "And my one heart is filled with him."

Again Black Elk indicated the pile of goods. The travois overflowed with new robes and furs, skins of soft kid leather, new tipi covers, highly prized white man's tobacco, bright wool blankets.

"What can *he* offer?" said Black Elk scornfully. "His brave love talk may move your heart. But it is buffalo robes which warm your cold bones! You are in love with a turncoat who fights white men's battles!"

"I cannot believe he is a turncoat," said Honey Eater. "He would not betray us! He would fight to the death for any Cheyenne in this tribe, including his enemies."

Black Elk fought hard to keep the rage from showing in his face. But his dark eyes snapped sparks at these words.

"You have sweet words for him! But you are still a child in these matters. Very well, we will wait until the report from River of Winds and Swift Canoe. Then we will wait no longer. You will announce your decision. Your war chief has spoken!"

Chapter Thirteen

Very early on the morning following the chase in the rocky basin, Touch the Sky and Little Horse briefly revisited the scene of their escape. Luck was with them: The whites had not found Touch the Sky's throwing axe. He spotted it in the trampled dirt and slipped it back into his legging sash. Then they rode the hidden game trails and long coulees which eventually connected with Hanchon property.

Touch the Sky wanted to talk to his father about last night's attempt to eavesdrop on Steele's men. The friends agreed that Little Horse would ride out near their former campsite to check the cottonwood for messages. Touch the Sky planned to ride close to his parents' house, then hobble the dun and sneak the rest of the way on foot. Even though the Hanchon wranglers had been told about him and the Bluecoats knew he was in the area, there was no sense alerting that Bluecoat sentry.

The Cheyennes agreed to meet again later that day back at their new camp on the hogback overlooking Steele's ranch. They split up at the rim of the Tongue River valley, Little Horse swinging up higher toward the rimrock, Touch the Sky descending into the fertile green quiltwork of the valley. Both riders stayed well into the trees and avoided skylining themselves or riding in the open.

Touch the Sky dismounted in the last belt of trees circling his parents' spread. From there he could see the mountains in the distance, aspen-gold in the lower elevations, still tipped white at their very summits with the snow that never melted. Between these majestic mountains and the verdant pastures, the foothills stretched out in ever-larger mounds that grew darker and seemed to shimmer in the distance. Dividing it all like a shiny strip of silver ribbon was the winding and looping river.

He hobbled the dun with rawhide and easily made his way to the house without being noticed by the yard sentry. It was still early enough to catch John Hanchon at the breakfast table.

"Well, maybe you didn't find out exactly when my horses are going in that corral," said Hanchon when Touch the Sky had finished telling his story. "But you gave Steele's gun-throwers one more proof that they aren't working for easy wages. Maybe they'll think twice before they steal them mustangs."

The optimism of his words was not reflected in his troubled eyes. Touch the Sky also noticed signs of increasing strain on his adopted mother's face. There were half circles of fatigue under her eyes, a new habit of glancing warily out of the kitchen window to see if any riders approached. He remembered a time when worry was a stranger to her face.

"Today," said Touch the Sky, "I'll move around Steele's place, keep an eye on his hands. If they're planning to move out tonight, there'll be signs of it. I don't think the strike, if one is planned, will be that soon, though. The corral isn't quite finished."

Later, as he rose from the table to leave, Sarah gripped both of his hands in hers.

"Son, listen to me. I want you and your friend to leave, leave soon. Oh, child, I'm so happy to see you again my heart could just fairly burst! But it's too dangerous for you here now. Soldiers are all around the area."

Touch the Sky glanced toward his father, expecting to see his mother's plea repeated in John Hanchon's face. Instead, Touch the Sky sensed the same feeling in his white father that he sensed in Little Horse: If a fight was unavoidable, they were keen for it. He had told his father what these men did to the Cheyenne people. *These men shed the blood of your own,* his father's eyes seemed to tell him now. *And if kin don't matter, what does? Law is slow and scarce out here, but justice must be swift and plenty.*

"We'll be all right," he assured his mother. He added proudly, "Don't worry about soldiers. I'm more likely to fall off my horse than get shot by one of *them*."

Despite his proud boast, Touch the Sky was worried. At the moment Hiram Steele and his white dogs had surprise on their side—only *they* knew the what and where and when of that new corral. He had to try again to learn something. He spied his opportunity on the way back from his parents' spread.

He was approaching the campsite from behind a line of cedar and scrub pine due west of Steele's main corral. Two wranglers were lashing the last corner posts for the new pole corral. All that remained to be finished after that was the gate, and new logs had been stacked nearby for that purpose.

These were two of Steele's regular hands, not from the bunch that rode with Abe Winslow. Touch the Sky recognized them from the days when he used to make deliveries out here. He gauged the terrain between the tree line, where he was hidden, and the worksite. Mostly tall horseweeds, with here and there an open patch of knee-high grass.

It would be risky, he knew as he stared at the rifles propped up against the corral fence near the two men. One of them also wore a sidearm. Touch the Sky decided his Sharps would be too awkward in the weeds, so he left it lashed to his pony.

At first he made good time low-crawling, timing his most rapid bursts with the stronger gusts of wind to cover his movement. As he neared the two workers, he was forced to slow down. Sharp pieces of flint dug into his elbows and knees, pesky flies bit his face. Soon he could hear the occasional sound of their voices, but he couldn't make out their words yet.

His senses fully alert for signs he'd been spotted, he quickly scuttled across an exposed stretch of shorter grass. Then he was back on his face again, inching closer to the corral.

"Well, still, if the scuttlebutt I hear is true, then it's goin' too far."

"Did I say it wasn't? No, sir! What I'm saying is this. You open your mouth about it, it's the last complaining you'll ever do. Old Hiram is over his head this time. He'll rue the day he ever threw in with Winslow and his bunch."

"I'll say! What Winslow brags he's got planned for the Innuns, it ain't Christian. A Christian will by God fight and kill an Innun if he's bound to. But he don't take pleasure in the kill, nor in talking about how he plans to carve up the body."

"Christian! Tim, you're behind times! These ain't no Christians."

"That's clear from what they got planned for the Hanchons."

Touch the Sky turned his head and focused all of his awareness on hearing what the two men said next. But at this point he felt the ground vibrating. Lifting his head slightly, he spotted several more hands riding toward the new corral from the main yard. It angered him to leave before he learned the all-important missing fact: *when* the next strike was coming. But he decided not to push his luck against the present odds.

He retreated to his dun and swung wide north, sticking well behind the trees. The things he had heard left his insides a welter of anger and fear. Whatever Steele and Winslow had planned for them all, it would be as cruel and brutal as the men themselves. His father bravely talked the he-bear talk. But how could two Cheyennes and a handful of horse-wranglers stop men like this—men who had the weight of the U.S. Army behind them?

Amidst this wild tumble of thoughts, his mind

kept showing him images of Kristen Steele, her wing-shaped eyes the seamless blue of endless summer sky. Perhaps these thoughts explained why he unconsciously nudged the dun closer and closer to a small pond well beyond the wagon track which ran past Steele's house.

Abruptly, he touched the pony's neck to halt her. As he looked, where the track seemed to disappear behind a series of grassy hummocks, memories were unleashed like floodwaters. Memories of meeting Kristen here in their secret copse behind the pond. Memories of long embraces, warm kisses, plans for their future in this new land that was like fruit ripe for picking.

Those were plans for his life as a white man, he reminded himself now. And they were a mistake. He was a Cheyenne and must always live like one.

Nonetheless, he hobbled the dun in a stand of cedar and, avoiding open stretches, approached the copse.

The wind chose this time to suddenly gust stronger, rustling the leaves around him and wrinkling the surface of the pond. Thus he did not hear the soft crying noises from within the copse.

He stepped through the close wall of pines and nearly tripped on Kristen!

"Matthew, oh, my God! You frightened me so!"

His face flushed warm. "I didn't know you were here, honest."

"It's not that. It's just, I can't believe you're here. Don't you know Pa's men will kill you on sight? You're not safe here!"

Her hair tumbled over her shoulders in a golden confusion. A white linen skirt was neatly tucked around her legs as she sat against the trunk of a huge walnut tree. Touch the Sky dropped to one knee beside her. A quick glance told him that the letters scattered around her were from him. Blushing and dropping her glance from his, she quickly gathered up the letters.

Her eyes were red and swollen from crying. "What is it?" he said.

She shook her head. "You're up against so much right now. It's not right to bother you with my troubles. Matthew, listen to me! Pa and his men will kill you in a minute if they spot you anywhere around here."

"Sure they will. I'm a Cheyenne, ain't I? That's good enough reason to most people."

"And it's wrong! It's just wrong, and I won't stand for it! That kind of senseless, mean hatred is why I will never marry Seth Carlson or any man like him! I don't care *what* Pa threatens!"

It was out now, so she told him about the encounter with her father and Seth Carlson and her father's declaration: Either she agreed to marry Carlson, or her father would ship her back East to live with his sister.

"Carlson!" Touch the Sky spat the word out of his mouth as if it were a bad taste. "He isn't worthy to kiss your boot, let alone marry you!"

"He's a horrible man! He hates what he's ordered to hate. He frightens me. There's this mean glint in his eye, sometimes, when he looks at me. The same glint he gets when he talks about Indians. He knows how I feel about you, and it galls him."

She stopped there, but Touch the Sky finished for her.

"Galls him that you love a Cheyenne instead of him?"

She nodded, another tear zigzagging down her cheek.

"Oh, Matthew, I'm so scared for you! Pa is at that stage where he doesn't raise his voice anymore. He just keeps getting quieter and more dangerous. I've seen it before, and when he gets this way, he always gets what he wants."

"He's already taken enough from me. This time he *won't* get what he wants."

Matthew dropped down beside her, one arm encircling her. She turned toward him and leaned against his bare chest, her hair soft and still sun warmed.

Swallowing hard so she could speak, Kristen said, "Do you still think about me?"

He nodded, not trusting his voice.

"Corey doesn't answer me when I ask him if you've got a girl—you know, a Cheyenne girl. But not answering, I guess that's a kind of answer."

Red men don't kiss their women, Touch the Sky reminded himself then as he smelled the clean honeysuckle smell of her skin. But he wanted to kiss her, and bad, and he could tell she wanted it too.

A horse whickered, close by on the wagon road, and Touch the Sky was on his feet in a blink.

He peered out past the brake of pines and across the pond. Four riders sat their horses, rifles propped across their saddletrees.

One was Abe Winslow, and he was staring toward the copse.

"C'mon, Abe!" called one of them good-naturedly. "You promised us two hours of hard drinking! Daylight's burning, Boss!"

"I'm tellin' you," said Winslowe, "I saw a redskin. Two of 'em, maybe more, I'm not certain there. It was sudden like, just in the corner of my eye. They was peekin' in at somethin' inside them trees."

"Well, they're gone now," said the other man. "We'll kill them later."

But Winslow urged his mount off the track and started around the pond. Silent but quick, Touch the Sky moved back beside Kristen.

"Pretend to be reading your letters," he whispered. "Just sit here and pretend to read."

Touch the Sky swung up into the sturdy lower branches of the walnut, trying not to shake them too much as he moved around to the back of the tree. He unsheathed his knife and held it ready in his teeth to free his grip.

Winslow reached the near end of the pond, halted, dismounted. Touch the Sky could watch him clearly through a tunnel in the leaves around him.

Winslow lifted his slouch hat long enough to give his head a good shake, throwing the filthy, wet-sand-colored hair back out of his eyes.

He drew a French-made grapeshot revolver from his sash. It was designed for close-range killing where aiming wasn't important and fired a 20-gauge shot load.

Touch the Sky transferred the knife from his teeth to his hand. Carefully, he maneuvered around until he was in position to spring out of the tree. But he could clearly see the other well-armed riders sitting on the far side of the pond, impatiently waiting.

"Christ Jesus, Abe!" one of them shouted. "I'm as dry as a year-old cow chip! We're working on Hiram Steele's time, what's your hurry?"

Even if he killed Winslow, there were three more

to fight—and Kristen sitting right there where lead would be flying!

"Easy," he whispered to Kristen. "Here he comes."

A few moments later Winslow stood inside the copse, staring at Kristen as if he'd just found a gold piece in the road.

"Yes?" she said archly. "Do you have a message from my father?"

Winslow grinned, baring green-rimmed teeth and gums the color of raw liver. "No need to play the quality miss with me, sugarplum. Some o' Hiram's wranglers already told me how you like them red bucks. No wonder they was peekin' in here—waitin' to see if it was their turn yet, I reckon."

It took a moment for his meaning to take. When it did, Kristen blushed to the roots of her hair and turned her face away.

"You are a filthy, disgusting pig," she said. "Leave me alone now or I'll tell my father."

Winslow laughed, brandishing the grapeshot revolver. "This here little gal will take care of your daddy quick, sweet corset. You remember that."

"Please leave me alone now!"

Winslow moved a step closer. Kristen seemed to shrink within herself, searching for more distance from him. Overhead, Touch the Sky silently began chanting a battle song, preparing himself to leap and kill in one smooth movement. He should be able to seize the grapeshot revolver before the other riders could react.

Winslow's voice had gone husky and intimate in a way that disgusted Kristen. "Tell me something, quality miss."

Now he stood towering over her. He leaned closer, his breath whistling in his nostrils. "Tell me this much. Is it true what I hear? I hear that a red man's jizzom is red too. Is that a fact? I mean, I figger you would know, bein' as how you meet with 'em out here."

Hatred welled up inside of Touch the Sky, raw and bitter and strong. But if he gave in to his urge to gut Winslow now, he endangered Kristen more than he already had. So he set his jaw hard, his mouth a straight, grim line, and held back. The moment to leap might yet come. And even as he thought these things, he wondered: Was Winslow just talking about her meetings with him, or just now had he actually spotted another Indian? Could it have been Little Horse? If so, why had Winslow mentioned there were two?

Kristen had turned her body protectively away from Winslow, refusing to meet his eyes. He laughed. He started to reach out to touch her hair.

Touch the Sky loosened his one-handed grip on the branch overhead, silently took in a long breath. *Between the fourth and fifth ribs,* he could hear Black Elk repeating. *That way it is straight to the heart. And you must twist as you thrust, tearing your enemy's guts.*

"Goddamnit, Abe!" shouted one of the men impatiently. "Are you draining your snake or what? We're ridin' on without you!"

He stared at the humiliated girl for another ten seconds or so. Then he turned and yelled to the men, "Hold your horses! I'm on my way!"

Then he looked down at Kristen again. "I'll be lookin' for you again out here. And you can tell that buck of yours his little trick in the basin was a big mistake. His scalp is gonna hang off my coup stick!"

"Brother, did you not see?" said Swift Canoe. "The white dog peered in, then left without firing! He spoke to Touch the Sky and the yellow-haired white woman. Yet during the raid in the basin, they pretended to be enemies. This white has joined in the treacherous plan to make it appear that Cheyennes are on the warpath against the white nation!"

River of Winds said nothing, his eyes lost in serious reflection. The two spies were hidden in a thicket behind the copse. They had carelessly come near to being captured when, engrossed in observing Touch the Sky and the white woman, they had not heard the white dogs approaching.

"Only think on these things," said Swift Canoe. "We have seen Touch the Sky and Little Horse receiving messages from Bluecoat pony soldiers. We saw the soldiers again riding to meet them on the ridge. Now we have seen this paleface speak with him. Are you finally sure in your heart, as I am, that they have turned against our people? Do you not see that they have agreed to play the fox, to make the whites believe that Cheyennes are on the warpath?"

Though he maintained his silence, River of Winds did indeed agree now that this was true. He was finally convinced when he saw Touch the Sky making love talk with the woman whose hair had trapped the sun. After all, everyone back at camp believed his heart belonged to Honey Eater.

"Little brother," he said finally, "now I am one with you in your belief. But we have no orders from the councillors. I will leave before our shadows are long in the sun and ride quickly back to the tribe with this news. You will remain here, all eyes and ears. But you will *not* raise your weapons against Touch the Sky, do you hear my words?"

"I hear them, and I will obey."

But deep in his heart, Swift Canoe felt only a deep loathing for this turncoat who had killed his brother and now sold his people for gold. He knew well that, despite the tribe's sanction against shedding Cheyenne blood, they would respect any brave who killed this terrible enemy of the red man.

He would watch, while River of Winds raced north, for his opportunity.

Chapter Fourteen

Tom Riley adjusted his hat a bit as the midday sun crept straight overhead. The recruit platoon of horse soldiers stood at parade rest for the noon formation, their faces dusty and sweatstreaked from morning maneuvers.

Riley had spent most of his time lately on training exercises north of Fort Bates—a recent change of assignment which he knew Seth Carlson had arranged to get him out of the picture. But now he and his unit had returned for supplies and remounts.

One thing Riley detested about garrison duty was the endless list of Department of the Army orders and directives he was forced to read aloud each day to his men. He finished off a long list now, his voice raw and tired from shouting out commands all morning.

"'Each year at this time,'" he read from a

sheaf of documents bearing the seal of the War Department, " 'the military is plagued with the same insidious problem at its frontier installations: those nefarious cowards sometimes known as snowbirds. These are unpatriotic men who join the Army during cold months for food and shelter, then desert with the arrival of spring.

" 'All legally enlisted men-in-arms are hereby advised: Snowbirds are also deserters, and if caught will be executed as enemies of their country.' "

"At least the Army kills you quick and clean," said one of the salty old NCO's who had fought in the Cherokee Wars back East. "Them goddamn Innuns'll cut off your peeder first!"

A few men laughed, but Riley let it go. They got enough harsh treatment from the likes of Seth Carlson.

He finished the latest batch of Army messages. Riley reminded the men of the regimental parade today at 1330 hours. Then he dismissed his men for their noon rations.

He was crossing the parade field, toward the bachelor officers' quarters behind the sutler's store, when Riley saw Hiram Steele ride through the main gate.

The big, broad-shouldered man sat straight in the saddle, looking neither to his left nor his right. His business often brought him to the fort. Riley knew it was not unusual for the rancher to visit the officer in charge of the stables, where he was apparently headed now. Nonetheless, Riley found himself swerving toward the complex of big, single-story buildings where the regiment's horses were stalled when not grazing.

He ducked behind the corner of a nearby barracks when Seth Carlson emerged from the Headquarters Building. The officer too headed toward the stables. He and Steele made a point of pretending not to notice each other.

Riley fell in behind a corporal marching a work detail and kept them between him and the stables until he'd crossed the parade field. Then, after confirming that Carlson and Steele were indeed meeting in one of the stable buildings, he hurried around behind it. A wooden loading arm protruded from the loft door, thick ropes dangling down. Riley gripped one of the ropes and climbed hand-over-hand up into the loft.

His boots silent in the thick-matted straw and hay, he crossed to the edge of the loft and glanced below. Normally a private or two would be cleaning out stalls or pounding caulks into horseshoes. But the soldiers had gone to the mess hall. Steele and Carlson stood near the stall where Carlson's new mount now chewed on a nose bag full of oats.

"How do you like him?" said Steele, nodding toward the strong, well-muscled chestnut he'd given the soldier to replace the black Carlson had been forced to shoot.

"I'm starting to think you *did* give me the best of your herd. He's fast and a strong jumper."

"That's an Indian-fighter's pony," said Steele proudly. "He's trained for steep slopes and mountain trails. That, and quick maneuvering. *This* animal would of sensed that prairie-dog hole and missed it."

"He'll get his first trial tonight."

"It's all set at your end then?" said Steele.

Carlson nodded. "It'll be me and three men from the dragoons, all of us in mufti. Now, I gave 'em my word: They're being paid to attack and burn the house and outbuildings, nothing else. We'll lay down cover fire on any wranglers in the yard, but it's up to your bunch to round up the horses and fight off Hanchon's men in the field. We have to hit quick and get the hell out."

Steele nodded. "If the redskin is around the house, he's yours. If he's out with the herds, Winslow can have him. I don't care who kills him, so long as he's put under. This strike will either break John Hanchon's will or kill him. I ain't out to kill him, mind you, just to drive him out of the mustang business. The choice is his."

"Speaking of choices," said Carlson, "has Kristen said anything more about—about what you talked about the other night? About us getting married?"

"She won't say boo to a goose since that night. She's stubborn and mule-headed just like her mother was. You want the straight, soldier? You or your men kill that Indian, hear? You kill that Indian, I'll by God make sure she marries you. Because, man to man, here's the way it is. Now *don't* mistake my meaning, we're in this thing together. But the plain truth is, I got a daughter that kisses redskins. And you are in love with a woman that's partial to a savage over you. We're both made fools of here. That Cheyenne is humiliating the pair of us."

Riley, peeking down over a bale of new hay, watched Carlson's smooth-shaven face set itself in hard, determined lines.

"I'll kill that red bastard, all right," he said, anger and jealousy clear in his tone.

One of the privates on work detail returned and the two men drifted out, still talking. Riley climbed back down from the loft and tried to order his confused thoughts. It was too late to place a message in the fork of the cottonwood for the Cheyennes. And Corey's place was an hour and a half's ride, the Hanchon spread at least an hour, two hours both ways.

The regimental parade was coming up in less than an hour. Harding was in love with the pomp and regulation and would never excuse him or any on-duty officer from leading his platoon through the drills. Any attempt to leave the fort now would draw suspicion, maybe even get him followed—thrown in the stockade, if Carlson got wind of it.

No. His best hope was to go through with the parade, turn his men over to the platoon sergeant immediately afterward, and then ride hard to the Hanchons with this new word, avoiding the sentry on Thompson's Bluff. He'd have to hope the raid was planned for some time late enough to permit establishing defenses.

Otherwise, the Hanchons were finished—if they survived with their lives. As for the Cheyennes, their fate was even clearer. They had no middle ground. They would either kill or be killed.

"So that's the long and the short of it, boys," said John Hanchon. "These aren't wranglers you'll be going up against, they're frontier hardcases used to cold-blooded killing. I can't rightly ask you to fight without telling you that. And I don't blame any man that walks out that door right now."

John Hanchon finished speaking and Touch the Sky felt a pall of awkward silence fall over the front parlor. The room was filled by an odd assemblage. The four remaining wranglers and

Wade McKenna, their boots crusted with dried mud from recent rains, stood nervously twisting their hats around in their hands. Tom Riley, still in uniform, stood slightly apart from them. On the far side of the room another little group was formed by Corey Robinson, Touch the Sky, and Little Horse. Sarah, over her loud protests, had been sent into Bighorn Falls to stay with Holly Miller, the seamstress.

Riley had ridden first to Corey's place, then dispatched the redhead to the Cheyennes' camp with the news. Little Horse had been reluctant to enter a lodge with so many whites. But he'd agreed when Touch the Sky said this paleface council was important. He listened carefully now while his friend interpreted the important bits of information. The wranglers occasionally aimed a curious glance toward them. The Cheyennes, however, carefully avoided any eye contact with them.

A hand named 'Braska Jones scratched his ear. Then he said, "I didn't sign on for no shootin' war. You're a good man, Mr. Hanchon, and that's God's own truth. I've put up with my share o' fightin'. But this tonight, this is gettin' down to the nut-cuttin'. I got family back in Omaha. I'll have to throw in my hand."

"Fair enough," said Hanchon. "You've been a good worker. I'll pay you off when we finish up here. Anybody else?"

"Ain't no mix of mine what 'Braska does," said Wade McKenna. "But young Riley here ain't from these parts neither, yet *he's* willing to put at 'em! The rest of us live in this valley. We've put down stakes and aim to stay. This ain't just your fight. Hell, I got plans for my own spread. We let Steele drive you under, none of us will be safe."

The other three hands nodded their approval of McKenna's words.

"All right then," said Hanchon. "It's settled. We don't know exactly when they're hitting us, just that it'll be well after dark. That means we go over the plan one time now and then just hunker down and wait. This is where I let a soldier take over."

Riley said, "There's nine of us total, counting me and Corey. Steele's regular hands will be busy rounding up and driving the horses. The shooting will be left to about a dozen mercenaries riding for Steele, and four soldiers who plan to attack the house and yard. I doubt if Steele himself will be riding.

"Me, John Hanchon, and you wranglers will ring the main herd behind cover. I'll direct fire. We'll be outnumbered, but they'll be riding in the open and expecting only a sleepy line rider or two to be out there. Shoot for their horses first so they'll be unable to cut out any mustangs."

Riley looked at Touch the Sky. They had already briefly discussed what the Cheyennes would do.

"These two are going to have the tough job," said Riley. "First of all, they'll be watching at Steele's spread when the riders head out. Then they'll get back to give us the word when and where the fight's coming to us. After that, they come back here and defend the house because the soldiers plan to attack right after the fight starts out in the pastures."

Riley turned to Corey. The youth had insisted on joining either the bunch in the pasture or the Cheyennes up at the house. But Riley had convinced him to perform a more important task.

"You, Corey, will ride back to the Steele spread. After Steele's men ride out, you're going to take that pole corral apart. If they do heist any mustangs, we'll make damn good and sure they got no place to put them. But watch out for any sentries while you're working."

Corey nodded.

"Everybody straight on the plan?" said John Hanchon.

McKenna and the hands nodded.

"Clean and check your weapons," said Riley. "There'll be a full moon, so stay covered down as much as possible. And remember, a rustler is useless on his feet. Shooting a horse is as good as shooting the man."

"I thank you all again," said Hanchon. "May God have mercy on all of us. It's going to be a hard fight."

"Brother," said Little Horse when the two Cheyennes were alone in the moonlit yard. "We are warriors and we cannot avoid this fight. But we have not dressed nor painted, we have made no sacrifice to the Arrows. And our sister has gone to her resting place in the west, leaving the sky to Uncle Moon."

Touch the Sky nodded, understanding. A Cheyenne was seldom considered a coward if he refused to fight after dark or without painting, so important were these things.

"We must try hard to avoid the kill," he said.

He glanced around the yard and the surrounding outbuildings, then considered the best possible approaches for attack. The most direct route from Fort Bates would be from the wagon track to the north. But the Bluecoat attackers would want to throw suspicion off the fort. Meaning the most probable direction of attack would be from the rim of the valley, down the long slope behind the house.

"Before we ride to spy on the white dogs," said Touch the Sky, "I will speak with my father. I think we should prepare more traps for our enemies."

But this talk of spying made him think again of something else. Something he had been worried about since hearing the tall, thin paleface named Winslow insist he'd seen two Indians peeking into that copse while he talked with Kristen.

He glanced carefully around, searching the blue-black twilight.

Little Horse saw him. "Still you fear the tribe has sent spies?"

Touch the Sky nodded. Little Horse too glanced carefully around. "I hope you are wrong, brother," he said. "Tonight we face a powerful enemy. We may die. If we have been declared enemies of our tribe, we cannot make the journey to the Land of Ghosts. We will be doomed to wander in the Forest of Tears alone forever."

"Then brother," said Touch the Sky, "let us make preparations, not words, for clearly we had better not die!"

Chapter Fifteen

Their preparations near the house complete, the two Cheyennes rode out together toward the Steele spread while the fat moon crept toward his zenith.

They stopped briefly at their hidden shelter on the hogback to prepare their weapons. Both Indians were silent now, absorbed in the silent task of preparing themselves for battle. They scooped clay out of the soil near the seep spring and darkened their exposed skin.

They were able to keep an eye on the house and main yard while they made these preparations. The first confirmation of the raid was the number of horses in the corral, many of which would normally have been stalled for the night by now. Steele's wranglers and Winslow's bunch, mostly keeping to themselves, stood in small groups smoking or checking their weapons.

The two Cheyennes crept downridge, moving even closer. Several times the door to the house swung open, and men would turn to look. Finally, when the two Cheyennes began to wonder if the strike was on after all, Hiram Steele stepped out into the buttery moonlight.

He nodded once, and Abe Winslow's rusted-hinge voice shouted out, "Grab leather, boys!"

The Cheyenne warriors quickly returned and untethered their ponies. Hugging the tree line, keeping a constant eye on the riders below, Touch the Sky and Little Horse tracked the marauders as they set out, riding two abreast strung out in pairs 50 feet apart—almost 20 men strong, a good-sized cavalry squad. But almost half of them were wranglers used to hard drinking and fistfights, not killing, Touch the Sky reminded himself.

Still, that left at least a dozen paid killers against Riley's force of six. Thus the Cheyennes wanted to learn more than just the exact time of attack—they needed to learn the approach route so the defenders could get in the best position. The initial moments of attack were the most important, Black Elk had reminded them constantly.

They held their ponies to a matching trot only until they were sure they knew the route—not down from the rim of the valley, but up from the coulees and defiles toward the main mustang herd in its summer pasture. The defenders would need to concentrate their fire at the open wall of the natural pen, through the coulee which approached it.

Once sure of this, the two red brothers nudged their ponies hard, pushing them recklessly but trusting them now after several sleeps of light duty. By now they had learned the swiftest routes through the valley. Soon they were well ahead of their enemy, long black locks streaming behind them as they urged their mounts even harder across open stretches of bottomland.

Touch the Sky quickly gave the word to his father and Tom Riley. Then, knowing time was stretching thin, the two Cheyennes raced toward the house. They hobbled their horses in protective thickets and moved into position, each kneeling behind sturdy young cedars behind the house. The trees grew near the bottom of the long slope leading down from the rimrock above.

This time they didn't have long to wait. The first rifle shots from the coulee told them the defenders had surprised Steele's riders. Soon a gun battle raged in earnest.

But the Cheyennes concentrated on the slope, where the silhouettes of four riders had just appeared at the crest.

Carlson was easy to recognize on the big chestnut Riley had told them about. All four riders wore civilian clothes. They fanned out slightly as they descended the slope, picking up speed until their mounts' hooves were hollow, rapid drumbeats.

When they were more than halfway down the slope, closing rapidly on the hidden Cheyennes, Touch the Sky snorted like a horse clearing its nose after a good drink. Little Horse snorted back, signaling that he was ready.

The riders bent low over their pommels, savagely spurring their mounts. The thundering grew louder. The Cheyennes could now make out divots of soil and grass flying as the strong cavalry horses tore up the ground.

At the last possible moment, when it seemed the riders were about to pass them, Touch the Sky jerked taut the rope stretched along the ground between his cedar and Little Horse's. With the rope lifted about three feet above the ground, he rapidly snubbed it around the cedar a few times to secure it.

One of the three dragoons rode a roan stallion. It hit the rope hard in mid-stride and tumbled forward fast, the rider's left arm snapping in two places when he landed on it. Moments later the panicked horse, struggling to regain its feet, planted a hoof square on the rider's chest and caved in his ribs as it righted itself and bolted back up the slope.

A ginger mustang carrying a second dragoon also went down, but less forcefully. Though the soldier was uninjured, his rifle was still in his saddle scabbard. The sight of his companion's crushed chest sent him fleeing in the direction of his mustang.

Carlson's fleet-footed chestnut and the remaining dragoon's powerful little Sioux-broken paint managed to leap at the last possible instant, clearing the rope. Intent on their mission, neither man slowed to check on their downed companions.

Carlson swerved toward the house, the mounted infantryman toward the bunkhouse. Both clutched rags soaked in kerosene and wrapped around sticks. The dragoon reached the bunkhouse first, halted his mount outside the door, slammed it open with a powerful thrust of his boot. The next moment he struck a sulphur match and the torch was ablaze. He flipped it inside the bunkhouse and headed toward the outlying stable, pulling another makeshift brand from his saddle pannier.

But Little Horse had raced into the yard behind the dragoon, staying out of sight. As the soldier, intent on lighting his second torch, slowed to burn the stable, Little Horse raced inside the bunkhouse and threw a mattress over the flaming brand.

He headed for the stable even as the dragoon raced about the yard with a third flaming torch, igniting hayricks. Hanchon had already told them not to worry about saving hay, just buildings.

It was Touch the Sky's job to deal with Seth Carlson. So far neither Carlson nor the dragoon was aware of the presence of the Cheyennes. With two hayricks flaming high, lighting up the house and yard like bright afternoon sun, they were slow to notice that the bunkhouse and stables were not engulfed in flames.

Carlson had reined in his horse before the house and lighted his torch. His arm was cocked back to throw it when two powerful hands gripped his left leg and jerked his foot from the stirrup. His right foot jerked free too, and a moment later he lay on his back in the dirt, the torch sputtering out.

The chestnut, spooked by the increasing flames in the yard and the sudden loss of its master, side-jumped hard and knocked Touch the Sky down before he could leap on Carlson. The officer was up on his knees, clawing his service pistol from its stiff leather holster, before Touch the Sky shook his head clear.

Carlson aimed, the Cheyenne leaped, the pistol spat fire as Touch the Sky slammed into him and bowled him over again.

They rolled once, twice, again in the dirt, grappling viciously. By the time Touch the Sky rolled on top of his opponent, there was a bright red crease of blood where the bullet had grazed the hollow just above his left hip.

The two archenemies fought like snarling wolves, ripping each other's skin, gouging eyes, even biting. The flames from the burning hayricks leaped and danced high into the sky all around them, casting eerie shadows as they fought.

So far Little Horse had managed to save all but the hayricks and one minor storage shack. Intent on defeating the dragoon without drawing blood, Little Horse was at first unaware that his companion was struggling for his life in the dirt.

Touch the Sky had strength and agility over the Bluecoat officer. But the pony soldier was heavier and had practiced the European style of wrestling while at West Point. Now he performed a deft little flip with his legs tensed, neatly tossing Touch the Sky aside.

Carlson's service Colt lay in the dirt several feet away, its primer cap spent. But now, as Touch the Sky scrambled after him again, the officer dipped a hand inside his tunic and came back out with a short-barreled .50-caliber hideout gun.

There was no time. Now he must either draw blood or die. But Touch the Sky was still resolved against killing at night, unpainted and unblessed by the Medicine Arrows.

Even as Carlson straightened his arm to fire, Touch the Sky snatched the knife from his sheath and flipped it at Carlson in one smooth, fluid movement. There was a sound like cloth ripping as the lethally honed blade sliced neatly into the wrist of the hand clutching the hideout gun.

The gun discharged its only slug, harmlessly sending it two feet over Touch the Sky's head. Carlson cried out in pain and clutched his wounded arm, too shocked to pull the knife back out. Touch the Sky picked up the service revolver and flung it far out into the yard.

"I am a better man than you, paleface!" said Touch the Sky. "Do you see that? You live now because I let you, white dog! The day is coming when we will meet on the true field of battle. And then your hair will dangle from my clout!"

Carlson yanked the knife free, almost fainting at the pain, and dropped it in the dirt. His wrist spuming blood, he turned quickly away and raced for his horse.

The yard was brilliantly lighted now as the hayricks crackled and sparked, shooting huge tongues of flame. But the house and main buildings were untouched, and this fact had drawn Abe Winslow's attention from the battle up at the pasture.

Things had fared badly for the attackers. They had been caught by surprise and several of his men were down, several more trapped. Steele's wranglers, spooked by all the flying lead, had taken to the hills or were crouched nearby in hiding. It was part of Steele's contingency plan that, should Winslow see that the house was not burning, he would ride down and do the deed Carlson had failed to do. Now, with lead flying thicker than trail dust, he was glad to get the hell out of there.

By now, between the noise of the flaming hayricks and the nickering horses in the main corral, Winslow was able to enter the yard unnoticed. Thus it was that, approaching Touch the Sky from behind, he saw the Indian defeat Carlson and send the officer packing.

Winslow slipped the grapeshot revolver from

his sash. He let his horse walk closer until he was at point-blank range. Then he aimed at the back of the Cheyenne's head.

"Brother, watch out!"

Winslow squeezed the trigger just as Little Horse's lance knocked his arm askew. The grape-shot revolver discharged its 20-gauge shot load with a deafening roar.

A moment later the dragoon, who had dismounted to pick up the carbine he had dropped, was sitting on the ground in shock and pain, gazing at the bloody stump of his left leg. The bone protruded like a shattered tree branch.

The soldier had never met Winslow. He had seen nothing. He knew only that this man now staring at him, smoking weapon in hand, had just blown his leg to hell and gone.

"You scum-sucking sonofabitch!" he snarled. And just before he passed out from pain and blood loss, he lifted his carbine, locked it into his hip socket, and sent a slug thwapping into Winslow's chest.

There was no time to rejoice in their victory at saving the house and driving off the attackers. Both Cheyennes made sure the flaming hay was in no danger of igniting buildings. Then they raced toward the high ground and the summer pasture, where the battle still raged. They were prepared to draw blood if necessary. But the shouts of encouragement from Hanchon's wranglers told them the fight went well.

"This is what I have seen, brothers and fathers. I did not ride south to condemn this tall stranger. But these are the things I have seen. I know this is a serious charge. But I believe in my heart that it is also a true charge. Touch the Sky and Little Horse are secretly aiding the Bluecoats! They are attacking paleface settlers under secret orders from a little soldier chief!"

River of Winds finished his long report and fell silent. His words left a shocked stillness in the council lodge. None was more troubled than old Arrow Keeper. Had this report come from Swift Canoe, he would have known it was delivered with more than one tongue. Swift Canoe's Wolverine Clan were known among the village as complainers who always shirked hard work and loved to stir up trouble.

But from River of Winds! Arrow Keeper trusted this brave's word and his keen sense of fair play. He would never speak in a wolf bark against another Cheyenne.

"I spoke straight-arrow all along!" said Wolf Who Hunts Smiling triumphantly. "He is not even a turncoat—he was a spy all along!"

The outburst of shouts from the younger warriors forced Arrow Keeper to fold his arms until it was silent.

"Brothers, hear your chief! I too am bothered by this word River of Winds brings. But still, much remains to be explained. If these two bucks are spies, then we must find out how this thing happened and how they have hurt us with our enemies. If they are innocent, we must give them opportunity to prove this thing."

River of Winds was instructed to join Swift Canoe again, then track the two Cheyennes, never letting them out of sight. River of Winds and Swift Canoe, Arrow Keeper insisted, must learn as much as possible about this dangerous alliance with pony soldiers.

Arrow Keeper was deeply troubled, and his concern was plain to the others. But deep in his heart he still resisted believing what was now obvious to all: that Touch the Sky and Little Horse had not only deserted their tribe for good, but were selling it out for gold. Arrow Keeper was well aware of the white man's ploy of creating "Indian attacks" to drum up war profits. Many Indians had already brought their tribes down for good with this treacherous service to the white profiteers.

The shaman was not surprised, after the council, to find Honey Eater anxiously waiting in front of his tipi.

"What was decided about Touch the Sky, Father?"

Honey Eater and everyone else in the tribe had already heard the charges against Touch the Sky and Little Horse—including the story about how he held a sun-haired paleface woman in his blanket and made love talk to her.

"Very little, daughter. The Headmen must learn more. These are very serious charges."

"Do *you* believe them?"

Arrow Keeper looked into the girl's agonized, hopeful eyes and felt a pang of remorse in his heart. "Honey Eater, I believe that River of Winds always speaks straight. I believe he saw what he tells us he saw. However, the meaning of what he has seen still eludes the tribe."

"But what else *can* it mean, when a Cheyenne holds a pretty young paleface woman in his arms? He prefers a blue-eyes over a Cheyenne!"

Arrow Keeper was forced to maintain silence. How could he dare build up the girl's expectations and risk ruining her chances for a good marriage? Time was running out for her. She would soon have to marry.

Reading all this in his troubled gaze, Honey Eater said, "Please tell me, Father, what do I do? Black Elk will wait no longer! Do I risk the anger of his clan again by sending the gift of horses back?"

Nothing in his medicine vision about Touch the Sky, Arrow Keeper reminded himself, predicted anything about a marriage to Honey Eater. All that was foretold was greatness for Touch the Sky as a war leader. Men who were marked for greatness were not always the best men to love.

Finally, his heart heavy, he said, "You must remember that you are a Cheyenne maiden. You must always do your duty, what is right for your tribe. Black Elk is a war leader who has been blooded for his tribe. He has many possessions, fine horses. True, he is perhaps too much tempered in the hard arts of warfare. But with the mellowing of age, he may also someday become a great peace chief. And he is respected by his people."

Honey Keeper nodded, though this was not what she wanted to hear. "Father," she repeated desperately, "should I become Black Elk's bride? Time has run out, he demands to know this day!"

But Arrow Keeper only shook his head, his face a mask of unreadable wrinkles.

"You must do your duty," he repeated.

"But is duty more important than my love?"

Again he shook his head. "Words are no good now, little one. Make your decision. Just remember: We live on through the will of the tribe. And the will of the tribe calls for you to marry Black Elk."

Chapter Sixteen

Today, thought Swift Canoe, *the turncoat named Touch the Sky will finally die.*

It had been four sleeps since the strange nighttime battle near the paleface lodge. While River of Winds made his report far to the north in Cheyenne country, Swift Canoe had watched the entire conflict unfold. The young Cheyenne had not, however, recognized the four Bluecoats without their soldier clothing. He assumed the clash was between white settlers only. And since Touch the Sky and Little Horse were still meeting with a young Bluecoat officer, clearly they were still the long knives' dogs even if they did cleverly defeat the raiders.

Swift Canoe lay behind a tree on the long ridge overlooking the Hanchon spread. For four sleeps now he had watched his fellow Cheyennes as they, in turn, continued to prowl about the territory between the two mustang ranches. But it appeared that they were finally ready to leave. Both were preparing to mount their ponies below, Touch the Sky speaking with the paleface man and woman who lived in the lodge.

Where, wondered Swift Canoe, would they ride to? Surely they were not treacherous enough to return to Yellow Bear's camp? Or was that part of the Bluecoat's orders to them?

River of Winds was due back shortly with their orders from the councillors. If he was going to finally do it, Swift Canoe told himself, it must be soon—this day. And against two such capable fighters as those two, he would get only one arrow off before he would be forced to flee for his life.

The Cheyenne who killed such an enemy of the tribe would earn the respect of many blooded warriors. It would not bloody the Medicine Arrows to kill a turncoat like Touch the Sky.

One arrow.

Swift Canoe checked the condition of his buffalo-sinew bowstring, selected the most perfectly fletched and balanced arrow from his quiver. He would wait until the turncoats' route was clear, then ride on ahead and find a good ambush point.

"I'm not sure *how* I feel about you leaving," Sarah Hanchon told her adopted Cheyenne son. "Part of me wants you right here like you used to be. The other part of me wants you away from here, where it's safer."

Touch the Sky nodded. He didn't want to admit that he too felt a similar confusion about where he belonged. Last night, in a dream, Honey Eater and Kristen had both turned into eagles who ripped him in half fighting over him.

"Actually," said John Hanchon, "it's safer around here thanks to the boys. At least for a while anyway. Best time to stay on, if they've a mind to."

The valley had been unnaturally quiet since the battle four days ago. The fight in the summer pasture had gone well for Riley and Hanchon. Most of Steele's wranglers had lit out, and many hadn't shown their faces in the valley since. With Winslow and several of his gun-throwers dead, the rest of the mercenaries had decided they had their bellyful of the Wyoming Territory.

But Touch the Sky had learned even better news through Tom Riley. Riley's letter, including copies of Carlson's falsified reports about Indian danger, had reached the territorial commander at Fort Laramie and drawn an instant response by special courier. Major Harding, red-faced at the reprimand he'd received from above, suddenly had a fire lit under him. He'd immediately complied with the order to form a special board of inquiry to look into the raids on the Hanchon spread.

Touch the Sky agreed with Riley—no charges were likely to be filed as a result of the inquiry. Steele had too much influence at the fort. But the simple knowledge that somebody was looking into it should give Steele pause to worry. More important, the irate territorial commander had insisted to Washington that a U.S. marshal and deputy be stationed at Bighorn Falls to handle civilian disputes. They were due to report for duty soon.

Seth Carlson, deemed grossly incompetent after

filing the inaccurate reports, had already been demoted to second lieutenant and reassigned to an even more desolate no-man's-land, the remote Army outpost called Fort Peck in the Montana Territory. Touch the Sky regretted not killing him. But at least he was nowhere near Kristen now.

To Little Horse, Touch the Sky translated Sarah's offer to stay. To his surprise, Little Horse smiled. He spoke in Cheyenne, asking Touch the Sky to translate. Touch the Sky was still surprised when he turned to his parents and told them:

"My friend says to tell you, 'My name is not War Eagle. It is Little Horse. Now I trust you to know it.' "

Sarah smiled at the smaller Cheyenne. Then, shyly, she pushed her son's black locks back off his forehead and said, "Matthew? You've never told your father and me your Cheyenne name. We want to know it."

For a moment he hesitated, self-conscious. He spoke the Cheyenne words and they repeated them several times.

"What does it mean?" asked Sarah.

"Touch the Sky," he replied.

The Hanchons both smiled at the same time. "I like it," said Sarah. "You certainly do measure up to it."

John Hanchon had given the two youths the weapons he'd lent them, along with plenty of ammunition in buckskin pouches. Their legging sashes were filled with dried meat and fruit for the journey north to the upcountry of the Powder. Sarah had thrown in a generous supply of the biscuits Little Horse loved. Corey had said good-bye earlier, stopping by with Tom Riley. If only, thought Touch the Sky, he could have had one more meeting with Kristen to say good-bye.

It felt like a nail was lodged in his throat when he finally told his parents it was time to ride. Sarah smiled brightly, but crystal teardrops beaded up on her lashes.

"The first time you left," she said, fighting to keep her voice under control, "you went out in the night and left us a note. I felt so empty and aching inside because I never got the chance to hug you good-bye. Now, I know you don't feel comfortable, a big strong Cheyenne being hugged by his mama! But you just step over here and give me that hug, Matthew or Touch the Sky or whoever my fine son is these days!"

He smiled and did as she requested, picking her right up off the ground and twirling her around. The gesture surprised Little Horse. Thinking it must be a white custom upon leave-taking, he too picked Sarah up and twirled her. He looked even more confused when the other three suddenly laughed at him.

John Hanchon folded one arm around Matthew, one around Little Horse. "We going to see you two again around here?"

Sarah looked at him, waiting hopefully for the right answer.

He didn't know what to say. He was a Cheyenne now, but making this journey might have cost him his place in the tribe. Arrow Keeper said a Cheyenne without a tribe was a dead man. But neither was it possible to make a life back here, where the white settlers refused to accept him.

"I don't know," he said honestly. "I don't know what's going to happen. If I can, you bet you'll see me again."

It wasn't the answer Sarah wanted, but it would have to do.

"Well, *we* plan on being here, son, thanks to you and Little Horse," said John Hanchon. "You two have a place here anytime you need it, the white homesteaders be damned! Keep your powder dry, boys!"

As Touch the Sky was about to swing onto his dun, Sarah ran close and hugged him again. Then, unable to control her sudden sobs, she raced off toward the house. When Touch the Sky turned to say his final farewell to his father, he was surprised to see that the older man's eyes were damp.

"We both love you, son," he said gruffly. "Now get on out of here before I make a damn fool of myself," he added. With a final wave of his thickly callused hand, he headed up toward the house to comfort his wife.

The two Cheyennes rode in silence for several minutes, pointing their mounts toward the northern rim of the valley. The elation of their recent victory had given way to the reality—they were riding back to an uncertain future.

Thinking these things, Touch the Sky glanced up toward the rimrock above them, scanned the thickly wooded slopes. Little Horse saw him and did the same. Both had been thinking the same thing since Abe Winslow claimed to have seen two Cheyennes who could not have been them: Whoever the council had sent to spy on them, they were good at their work. Were they perhaps two more of Black Elk's well-trained warriors?

These two, thought Swift Canoe incredulously, were as brazen as magpies! It appeared that they were actually heading back toward the Cheyenne camp.

Sure of the route they would follow for a while now, he untethered his pony and raced ahead until he reached a good vantage point where the trail curved around a huge shoulder of rock strata. He hobbled his pony well back behind the protruding formation so he'd be ready to flee. Then, climbing the rock shelves like stairs, he made his way to the top of the shoulder.

Perfect. He could see the land for miles and miles from here, and the two riders winding their way slowly closer.

He lay on his belly on the warm rock. He slipped the selected arrow from his quiver, lined the notch up with his bowstring. Then he held it down at the ready, waiting patiently, his face as blank and impassive as the rock he lay on.

The two Cheyennes were about to draw abreast of a huge stratified rock shoulder when Little Horse suddenly said, "Brother! Someone approaches!"

They nudged their ponies off the trail and into the thickets, then dismounted. Touch the Sky unlashed the Sharps and made sure a primer cap and bullet were loaded.

Again, Touch the Sky heard nothing at first, another proof of Little Horse's keen hearing. Then, faintly, he detected the lazy clip-clop of shod hooves. He slipped his finger inside the trigger guard and took up the slack, waiting.

A moment later Kristen rode around the bend on her swayback piebald.

"Wait here," he told Little Horse, his heart swelling into his throat and making words difficult.

Kristen's surprise, when he stepped out and caught the bridle of her horse, quickly turned to joy at seeing him.

"I was hoping to meet you! Corey told me you were leaving. Oh, Matthew, I just had to say good-bye!"

He helped her dismount, his eyes unable to feast enough on her spun-gold masses of hair and flawless white skin.

"I knew you couldn't come to my place, and I didn't want to risk riling Pa by getting caught coming to your parents' spread again. So I asked Corey which route you'd be likely to take."

"How is your pa treating you?" said Matthew.

"Things are better. He's been a little more humble since a bunch of his own hands quit on him after that raid. The idea of this U.S. marshal coming has got him worried. And Matthew? He *knows* I know. I confronted him with everything about what he tried to do to your mother and father. It's shamed him enough that he wants to make peace with me."

"But will he stay this way?"

Her pretty face was creased by a frown. Touch the Sky realized that her answer was the same one he had just given his mother.

"I don't know. I just don't know what's going to happen."

Tentatively, she reached one finger out and touched the mass of burn scar on his bare, flat, tautly muscled stomach.

"Matthew? Do you love the woman you're riding back to more than you love me?"

The question took him by surprise and left him without words. For a moment he recalled that dream again, Honey Eater and Kristen fighting over him, literally tearing him in two, a piece for each world. He opened his mouth to answer when she suddenly raised one hand to his lips.

"Shush! Never mind, I don't want to know. Just remember this. I love you! I know it's impossible and all wrong, but I love you! Matthew, I can't predict Pa's moods. Do you understand me? I don't know how long I'm even going to be living here. If he throws me out, I'll probably never see you again. I can't stand that thought!"

She could no longer speak. Tears streaming down her face, she reached up on tiptoe and kissed his lips. Then, doing it so quickly he didn't even have time to assist her, she mounted and rode back in the direction she'd come, pushing the piebald to a surprisingly lively pace.

Touch the Sky watched her disappear, her kiss still lingering like a gentle touch on his lips. He was about to turn toward the thickets when, again, he had the sudden feeling he was being watched.

He glanced all around, unable to see much because of the huge rock formation beside him which loomed over him like a wide tower, blocking the sun. But the feeling was still there like a hand on the back of his neck. If the tribe had indeed sent spies, what did this mean?

He stepped across the trail. Little Horse stepped out to meet him, leading their ponies. Touch the Sky's eye caught something bright glittering in the dirt. He stopped, glanced down.

A blue silk ribbon. Kristen must have dropped it.

A heartbeat after he crouched down to pick it up, an arrow missed his head by inches and embedded itself firmly in the trunk of the aspen beside him. It struck so hard that the shaft was buried almost two inches into the trunk.

Despite the shock of it, neither Cheyenne moved for several long moments. Then they briefly examined the arrow and locked glances.

Neither brave was surprised to recognize Cheyenne markings.

Even when they heard a pony escaping behind the rock shoulder, they didn't bother to give chase. This close to the soldiertown of Fort Bates was no place for Cheyennes to be warring against each other. And neither warrior was interested in revenge at that moment. Revenge was a small thing in the face of the possible banishment or even execution which might await them at the Powder River camp.

"Brother," said Little Horse, his voice reverent with wonder, "that arrow should have put you under. But I have seen another arrow, the one buried in your hair. You were not meant to die just then because the hand of the supernatural is in this thing."

His mouth set in its grim, determined slit, Touch the Sky snapped the arrow in half and threw it into the thickets. He and Little Horse had fought honorably, following the Cheyenne way. They had at least given his white parents a fighting chance to survive in the valley. It was right to come here and fight.

But returning to his old life, seeing Kristen again, had once again left him feeling like a man with a foot planted in two worlds, unsure which one was his. And as they rode, gazing uneasily around, that broken arrow became an omen of the unknown fate which awaited them upon their return.